0.001 km/h

 1 km/h

 12 km/h

 17 km/h

 30 km/h

 32 km/h

 44 km/h

 48 km/h

 56 km/h

 56 km/h

 67 km/h

 80 km/h

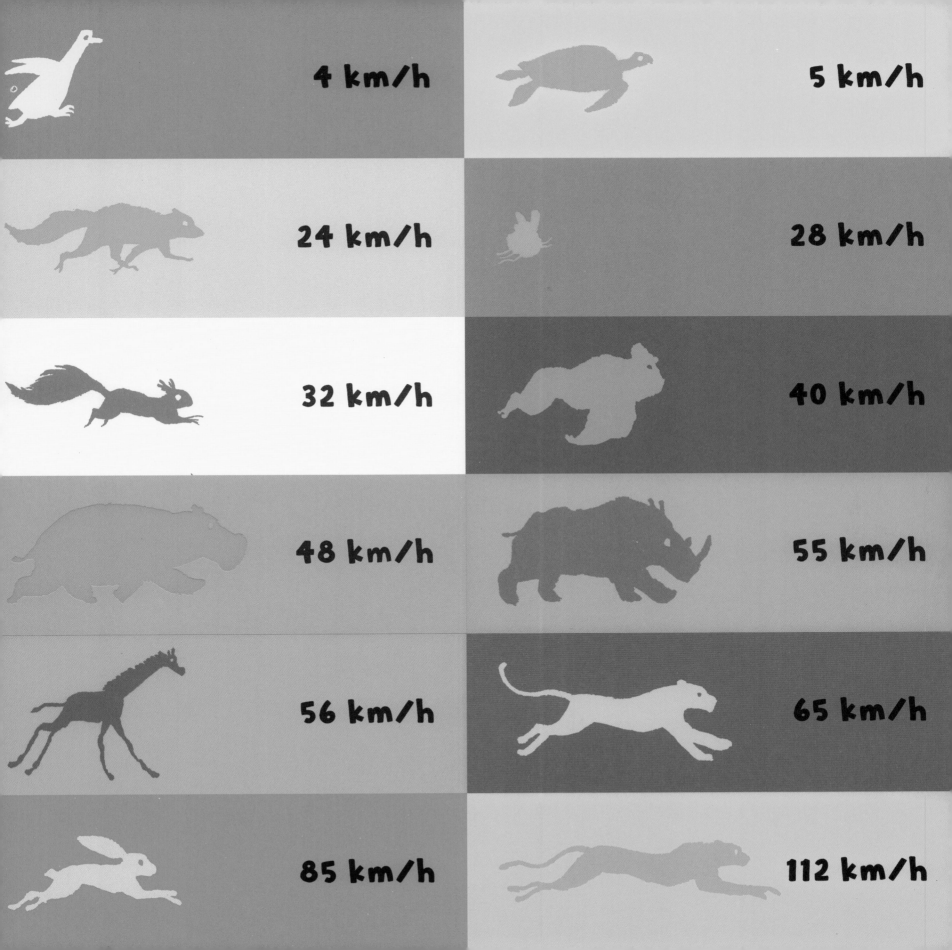

4 km/h

5 km/h

24 km/h

28 km/h

32 km/h

40 km/h

48 km/h

55 km/h

56 km/h

65 km/h

85 km/h

112 km/h

For Jodie – T.N.

For Dana – R.C.

First published 2023 by Macmillan Children's Books
an imprint of Pan Macmillan

The Smithson, 6 Briset Street, London EC1M 5NR
EU representative: Macmillan Publishers Ireland Limited,
1st Floor, The Liffey Trust Centre, 117–126 Sheriff Street Upper,
Dublin 1, D01 YC43
Associated companies throughout the world

www.panmacmillan.com

Hardback ISBN: 978-1-5290-6054-6
Paperback ISBN: 978-1-5290-6055-3

Text copyright © Tom Nicoll 2023
Illustrations copyright © Ross Collins 2023

1 3 5 7 9 8 6 4 2

A CIP catalogue record for this book is available from the British Library.

Printed in China.

TOM NICOLL and ROSS COLLINS
THERE'S NOTHING FASTER than a CHEETAH

MACMILLAN CHILDREN'S BOOKS

A race? How exciting!
But who's that on the
starting line?

The small one is a snail
and the cheeky looking
one is a cheetah.

But don't get too excited.

Snails are *too* slow to
chase cheetahs.

In fact, there's NOTHING
faster than a cheetah!

Nothing?

NOTHING

Penguins on pogo sticks?

NO WAY!

A buffalo on a bicycle?

SORRY.

What about a hippo
in a hang-glider?

NOT A CHANCE.

A giraffe in a jetpack?

That's a TALL ORDER.

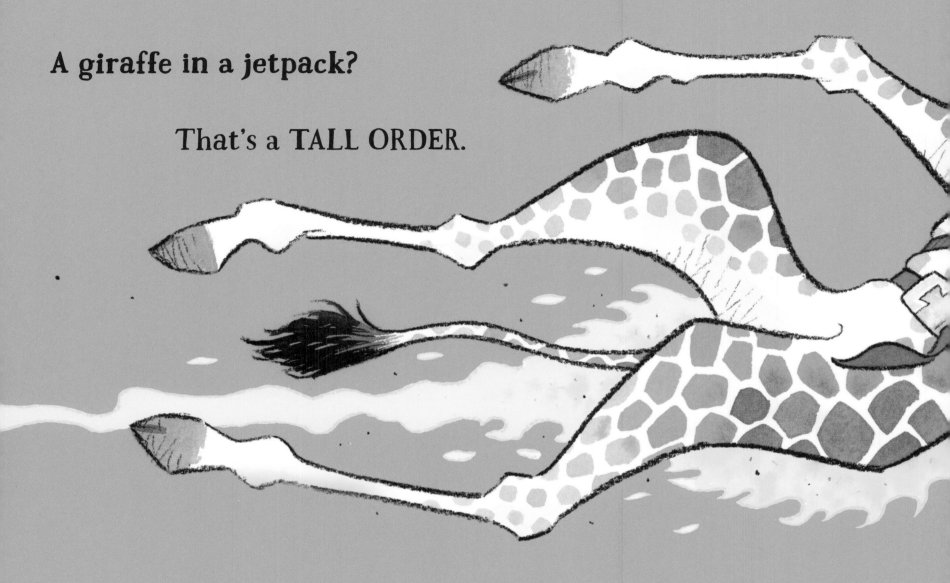

How about some mice on motorbikes?

She'll make
SHORT WORK
of them.

Surely a lion in a lorry at least has a chance?

You'd think so, but NO.

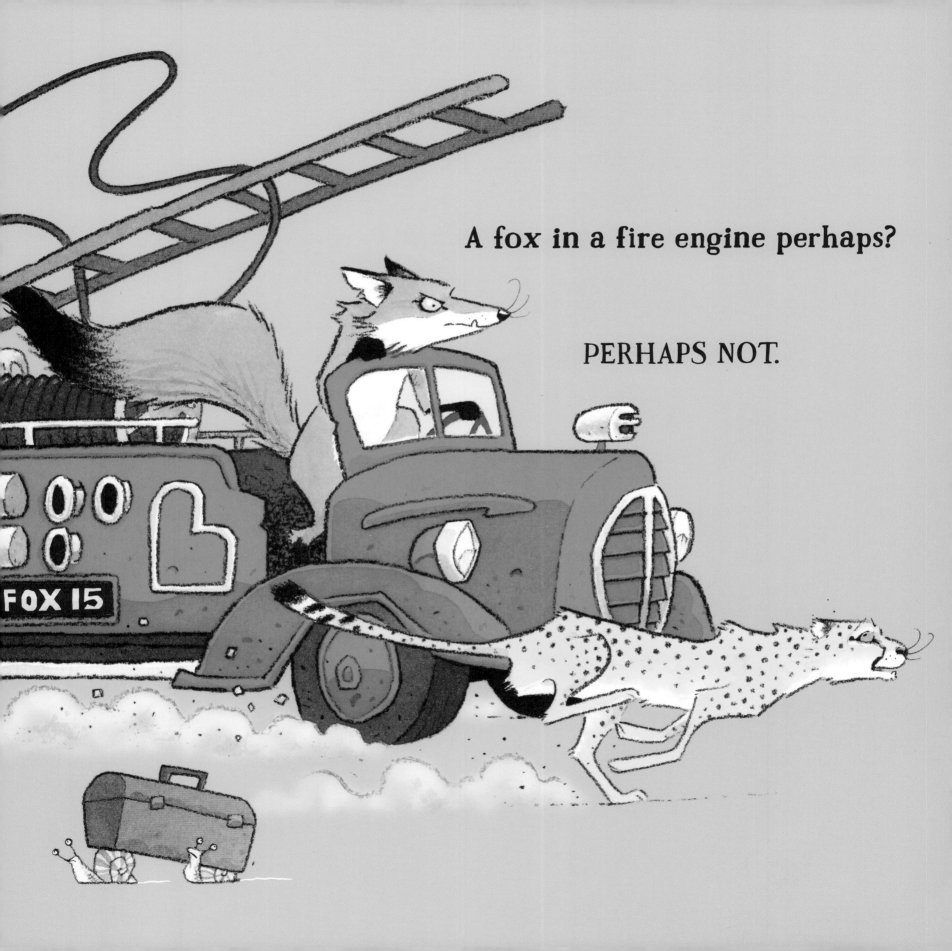

I know: a crocodile in a campervan!

He can't keep up.

A bear on a beach buggy?

Barely a bother.

Is cheetah ok? She looks exhausted . . .

She's fine. Just a little tired from trouncing a tortoise, a tiger and two turtles in a taxi.

Are you sure?
Maybe she should take a break?

And lose to some squirrels
on snowmobiles?

NO THANK YOU!

Those gorillas in go-karts are gaining on her.

I've told you NOTHING is faster than a cheetah!

INCLUDING bees and badgers and beagles on buses?

ESPECIALLY bees and badgers and beagles on buses.

He came closer than most.

A rabbit in a rocket? SURELY ...

NO not even that.

Then that's it. I guess NOTHING
is faster than a cheetah!

Didn't I tell you that?
Well, perhaps just one thing...

WHAT? What could possibly be faster than a cheetah?

The ONLY thing faster than a cheetah is...

... Seventeen sneaky snails stuck to a self-made, seriously silly, supersonic, steam-powered skateboard!

 0.001 km/h

 1 km/h

 12 km/h

 17 km/h

 30 km/h

 32 km/h

 48 km/h

 48 km/h

 56 km/h

 56 km/h

 80 km/h

 85 km/h

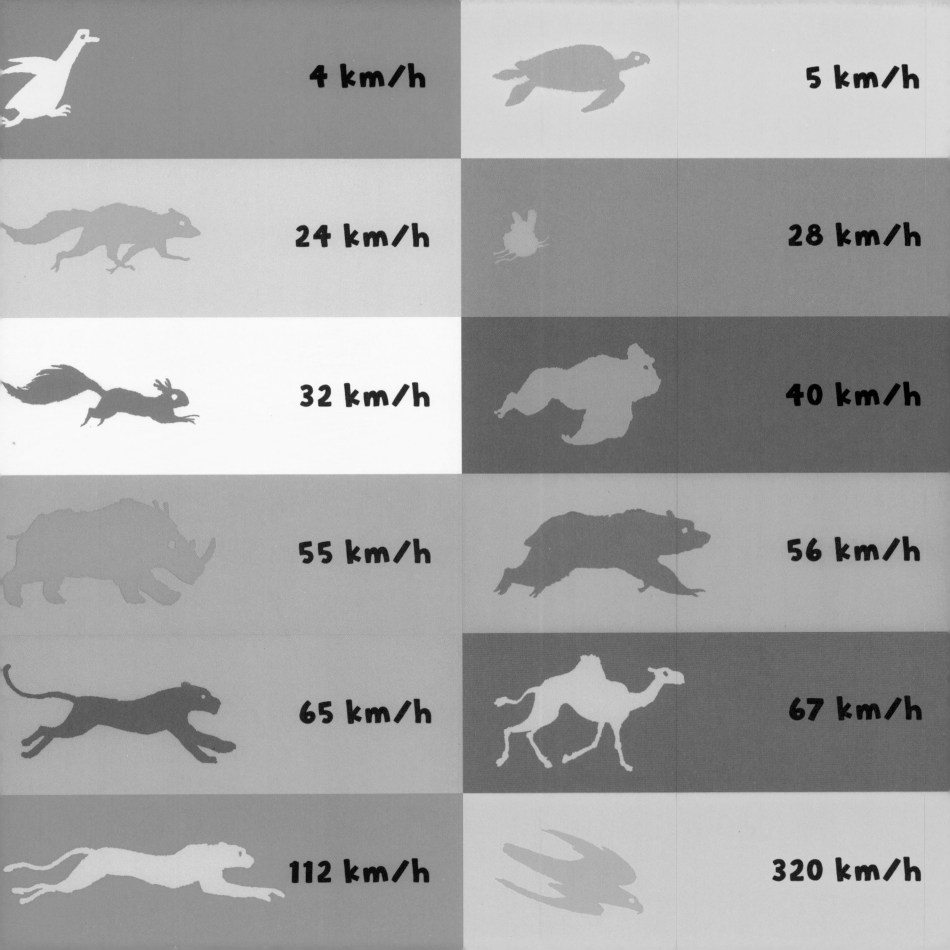

4 km/h

5 km/h

24 km/h

28 km/h

32 km/h

40 km/h

55 km/h

56 km/h

65 km/h

67 km/h

112 km/h

320 km/h

Community Service, Social Education and the Curriculum

British Library Cataloguing in Publication Data

361 (42) Scv.

Peter Scrimshaw

Scrimshaw, Peter
    Community service, social education and
the curriculum.
    1. Social group work in education
    2. Study and teaching
    3. Students — Great Britain — Social conditions
        I. Title
    361.7'2   LC221

ISBN 0 340 26363 8

First published 1981

HODDER AND STOUGHTON
LONDON SYDNEY AUCKLAND TORONTO

British Library Cataloguing in Publication Data

Scrimshaw, Peter
 Community service, social education and
 the curriculum.
 1. Social group work—Great Britain
 —Study and teaching
 2. Student Volunteers in social service—
 Great Britain
 I. Title
 361.3'7 HV245

 ISBN 0 340 24450 X

First published 1981

Printed and bound in Great Britain for
Hodder and Stoughton Educational,
a division of Hodder and Stoughton Ltd,
Mill Road, Dunton Green, Sevenoaks, Kent,
by Clarke, Doble and Brendon Ltd, Plymouth.

CONTENTS

CONTENTS

ACKNOWLEDGMENTS

This book would have been impossible to produce without the active cooperation of a large number of people. The Education and Social Services Departments of the Cambridgeshire Local Authority jointly funded the project discussed in Chapters I to IV, and paid my personal expenses in connection with the research required for the report on which those chapters are based. The Cambridge Institute of Education provided the reprographic and secretarial assistance needed to produce the report at no charge, and with the absolute minimum of administrative commotion. Charles Beresford and other staff at the Homerton Teachers' Centre, Cambridge also provided various kinds of unobtrusive support, for which I am grateful.

Numerous pupils and staff from Chesterton and Swavesey Schools and Impington Village College, together with members of the Homerton Study Group, went to considerable trouble to provide material for that report, knowing that it might be highly critical of what they were trying to achieve. My debt to all of them is considerable.

Preparation of the book itself was made possible only by the willingness of the Authority and the Heads and Warden of the schools concerned to give me permission to use the material in the original report as the basis for the first four chapters of the book.

I would like to express my particular thanks to Ivy Sheldon of the Cambridge Institute and Viv Burrows of the Faculty of Educational Studies at the Open University. Their task in preparing transcripts, the original report and the typescript for the book has been a considerable one. The efficiency, tolerance and good humour with which they dealt with that work has made the job very much easier than it would otherwise have been.

Finally, a special word of thanks to Pat, Clare and Diarmid who in their very different ways have continually reminded me of what Educational Theory should be about. This book is dedicated to them.

PREFACE

This book has been written with two main groups of readers in mind. The first consists of those both inside and outside schools who are actively working to promote community service programmes as part of the curriculum. The second consists of teachers (especially in senior positions) who have some cautious sympathy with the potential contribution that community service work might make to social education in school. Such teachers are often (in my view rightly) concerned to get a clearer picture of the problems and possibilities the work creates before deciding whether or not to commit themselves to active support for it. In addition I hope the book will be of some interest to those (both in schools and out of them) with a general concern for relating curriculum theory to school practice, to the ultimate benefit of both.

The first four chapters are an analytical study of community service programmes in three Cambridgeshire schools. In those chapters no attempt has been made to pass judgment upon the activities of the schools or indeed upon the general desirability of including community service work in the curriculum, but only to make visible something of the variety and complexity of such programmes and their effects.

The substance of that part of the book was drawn from an LEA sponsored report in 1977. In the course of preparing it I came across a certain amount of general information about how the community service movement had developed nationally and how some of its supporters envisaged its role in schools. It also became increasingly clear to me that it was impossible to give any satisfactory account of community service work as a curriculum innovation without locating it within some view of social education as a whole. This in turn could only be understood by being set against the background of post-war changes in society and in the responses of secondary schools to those changes. The second half of the book offers an account of these matters.

For a variety of reasons which are made clear in the book, community service work is not a curriculum innovation that can be presented to schools in any neatly packaged way, complete with predictable outcomes. Both the form it takes within a school and its effects upon both pupils and the rest of the curriculum depend very much upon the organisation and ethos of the school and the social context within which it works. This presents a considerable problem to an author who believes that the value of a piece of curriculum research must ultimately rest upon its contributing to the improvement of education in the school.

I have attempted to resolve this problem by emphasising throughout the tentative (and indeed often largely speculative) nature of the account being offered. What the account provides is a set of hypotheses for readers to test against their own experience, not a set of conclusions to be applied. I would welcome comments from readers on the practical value of the book, and especially on any points where they find its treatment of particular issues inadequate or unhelpful. Such comments can be sent to me at:

The Faculty of Educational Studies,
The Open University,
Walton Hall,
Milton Keynes,
Buckinghamshire.
MK7 6AA

Peter Scrimshaw

Part One: The Cambridgeshire Community Study/Service Project

CHAPTER I

THE STUDY

Early in 1972 a local working party was formed in Cambridge, made up of teachers and others who wished to develop community service work in local schools. With some support from a few officers within the Cambridgeshire LEA, the group prepared a variety of proposals and background papers urging that community service programmes should be given positive encouragement by the Authority. For a variety of reasons, notably the problems created by local government reorganisation, there was little immediate response from the Authority. In the meantime, however, what became known as the Homerton Study Group continued to encourage work in local schools.

In March 1975 it was agreed that a special allocation of funds should be made available to three schools to enable them to maintain what came to be called Community Study/Service (or CSS) programmes over a two-year period. It was also decided to appoint an outside consultant to prepare an independent report upon the problems and possibilities that such work presented, as revealed by the programmes being pursued in the three schools concerned.

The original consultant was obliged to withdraw at an early stage, having been appointed to a Chair in Northern Ireland. At the request of the Authority I took over respons-

ibility for the independent report in the summer of 1975, with the autumn of 1977 as the agreed target date for submission. The purpose of the report, as laid down in the contract between the consultant and the Authority, was to assist the Authority in deciding upon its general policy in relation to school-based community service work. In order to gain the material for the report I interviewed sixteen members of staff individually in the schools, three Youth Action organisers and some forty pupils, individually or in small groups. I also observed the meetings of the Homerton Study Group over a period of two years, and collected written material of various kinds relevant to the programmes.

Despite some serious methodological weaknesses, the study provided a fair amount of material concerning the possibilities of school-based community service work and some of the problems that it can present for schools. With the permission of the LEA and the schools concerned the bulk of Part One of this book is based upon that material. However, before we look at what emerged from the study some brief comments on the schools and the LEA may help the reader to set the findings in their context.

At the time that the study was carried out Cambridgeshire LEA itself had just begun to settle down after a major local government reorganisation, which had created a new and much enlarged local authority. However the majority of the schools represented in the Homerton Study Group were within the area of the old Cambridgeshire Authority.

One significant point about this was that they had therefore potentially been influenced by the ideas and policies of Henry Morris, who had been Chief Education Officer for Cambridgeshire from 1922 to 1954.[1] Morris had gained a national reputation for his advocacy of closer links between rural secondary schools and the social and cultural life of the surrounding community. These links had been given concrete expression in the creation of a number of Village Colleges. In these Colleges, schooling, community activities and various kinds of social provision were to be made available within one set of buildings. By this means Morris hoped to create increased facilities and opportunities for people of all ages within the rural areas served by the colleges, and to strengthen the sense of community within such areas.[2]

Two of the three Project schools, namely Impington and Swavesey, were in fact Village Colleges. The first serves an area around a large village that is now effectively on the outskirts of Cambridge itself; the second is some sixteen kilometres from the city. Both of these schools thus had a tradition of community links that may have partly explained and supported their interest in community service work. On a more concrete level, both schools had tutors attached to them with special responsibilities for the development of youth and community work in the area. In both schools responsibility for staffing the community service programmes was shared between teachers and tutors. For the sake of brevity I will subsequently refer to staff in both categories as tutors.

Chesterton, the third Project school, is located within Cambridge itself, serving a mixed housing area in the north-eastern sector of the city. It was originally designed as two single sex schools built side by side on the same site.

All three schools had effectively begun life as secondary moderns being quite heavily 'creamed' by the public and private sector selective schools located in Cambridge. At the time of the study all three had begun the transformation into comprehensives. However the Fourth and Fifth Year groups (with which the study was mainly concerned) were still largely made up of former secondary modern pupils.

The other major distinctive feature of the situation was the existence in Cambridge of a branch of Youth Action with two full-time organisers.[3] Youth Action is one of a number of national voluntary organisations set up to assist both young volunteers and school-based groups to engage in community service work. One of the Youth Action organisers had been prominent in the setting up of the Homerton Study Group, and the organisation channelled many requests for help from the community to schools known to have community service programmes.

The three schools, then, were in certain respects somewhat better placed than most to sustain their current CSS work. There was some short-term financial support available, the programmes were already established, and Youth Action was providing a partial source of jobs for the schools. However it is important to note that these advantages were not in any way extraordinary.

Furthermore the purpose of the Project was not to give the schools concerned exceptional sources of outside advice or encouragement. Like other schools in the area they had one or two staff attending the termly meetings of the Study Group, but this provided no more help than any teacher study group would do. By agreement,[4] the independent consultant did not offer any comments during the two year period on the work going on in the schools, nor act as a transmitter of ideas or suggestions either within the schools or between them.

Rather what was attempted was to gather information and views about three ongoing programmes and from this material to try to identify some features that looked as though they might be of some general relevance to schools interested in community service work. For this reason, and also in order to protect individual schools from any criticism, all the data in the report was presented in a way that concealed the identity of individuals and their schools from outsiders. Although this automatically meant some loss in the value of the report, it arguably went some way towards ensuring that nobody interviewed felt any need to conceal problems or over-emphasise successes. With this background in mind, let us turn now to the findings that emerged from the study.

References

1 See Rée for a biographical study of Morris and his influence upon the educational system in Cambridgeshire.
2 His proposals are summarised in his paper 'The Village College'.
3 A short history of Youth Action, Cambridge is now available; see Woodward.
4 The contract between the LEA and myself is reproduced in the Appendix (p. 81). It represented an attempt to formulate a relationship between the external researcher and the Study Group that would produce what I have elsewhere (Scrimshaw 1979) described as a joint evaluation.

CHAPTER II

ANALYSING COMMUNITY STUDY/ SERVICE PROGRAMMES

The first point to make about analysing the role of community service work in schools is that it cannot be considered in isolation from the rest of the school's work. This is not only because any programme in a secondary school is indirectly affected by other activities. In the case of community service there are often much closer links, as the work may be more or less firmly integrated into some wider course or set of courses, involving study elements related in some way to the visits themselves.

In investigating the work there was a need to look at a variety of types of programme. These fell upon a spectrum, ranging from some in which the service element made up virtually the whole programme, through to others where a minimal amount of community service appeared in what was essentially a classroom-based course of study of one kind or another. The rather clumsy, but accurate phrase 'Community Study/Service' (or CSS for short) was adopted as a generic title for courses or programmes falling anywhere within this spectrum of possibilities.

This chapter will be concerned to look at some of the aims proposed for CSS by members of the Study Group, to identify some of the major respects in which CSS programmes may vary, and to indicate what appeared to be the most important practical considerations that arose in relation to these variations.

Because community service is the label for an activity rather than for a body of knowledge or skills, there are fewer constraints upon the purposes for which schools might take up the

activity than is usual. On the face of it, one might assume that its rationale would be that it provided a service to the community. However, for curricular purposes this account is too simple. Firstly it neither specifies who precisely is to be served, or what constitutes 'service' in this context. Secondly, it does not explain why schools as such should be involved in the activity at all — for they are generally expected to be organisations largely devoted to educating their members, not a branch of the voluntary social services.

However, this is to assume that an activity can only have one useful purpose, rather than several. Yet it is commonly the case in schools that a programme is designed to produce simultaneously a range of benefits of various kinds. Where CSS is unusual (although not unique) is that the valuable outcomes that it might try to produce can include benefits for people outside the school, as well as educational benefits for the pupils themselves.

In order to get some picture of the range of aims that CSS might have, the members of the Study Group were asked for their views on this, using a short questionnaire. This asked them to indicate what they saw as the potential benefits that the existence of a CSS programme might be intended to provide for various groups concerned. These were categorised as:

benefits to the pupils involved in the
programme
benefits to members of the community
outside the school
benefits to the school as an institution

benefits to other people
benefits to teachers

The half-dozen replies received indicated that, even within that small and self-selected group, there was quite a wide variety of views on what community service in schools might be intended to achieve.

Within this particular group, benefits to the pupils were commonly seen in terms of the moral, emotional or character development of the pupils, with the growth of a sense of responsibility, sympathy for others and personal self-respect often being mentioned:

'CSS can provide for the development of responsibility, confidence, emotional maturity and altruistic and caring attitudes.'
(Organiser)

'It can give dignity to being a pupil at school and growing self-respect through respect for others.' (Head)

Cognitive aims were also often mentioned. Here the emphasis was upon gaining knowledge of the community, of the needs of others and (occasionally) self-knowledge.

' ... to involve children (in) the realisation that there is another world besides their homes and the four walls of the school.'
(Tutor)

'Enabling them to see their personal problems in perspective.'
(Organiser)

'The exercise of their sympathetic imagination to put themselves into someone else's shoes.' (Head)

In addition there were occasional references to the career information aspects of such work, plus some general concern that pupils should develop and practice manual and communication skills and (from one tutor) the suggestion that it offered them an alternative to academic studies for part of the week.

Benefits to members of the community outside school were usually expressed in terms of the direct practical value of the work done to the recipients. There was also some concern that the attitudes of the community towards the young should be improved.

The hope was frequently expressed that community service programmes would improve the relationship between the school and the local community. There was also a belief that relationships within the school would gain from the existence of such a programme.

'To help within the school, e.g. remedial work, charity collections.' (Tutor)

'To foster the sense that we as a school are helped by our community and can in turn help it.' (Tutor)

'I think some Heads want to do it because they think it might give their schools a good image. Some Heads don't want to do it because they think, as (a Head) puts it: "The parents think we are only doing this because we can't do Education proper".' (Organiser)

'One thing which I would like to see broken down is the image of youth as unconcerned and as a very selfish group in our society.'
(Organiser)

There was a very mixed spread of views that indicated a concern for benefits to pupils not taking the programme.

'Demonstrating to non-involved pupils that the school is open to the community in which it is set.' (Organiser)

'Providing a field of activity in which the more and less able can work together on equal terms.' (Organiser)

'An influential effect for good upon the mass (i.e. of other pupils) by report from the practitioners.' (Head)

The possible benefits to teachers were hardly mentioned at all, although one organiser commented that teachers did the work because they enjoyed it.

Reflection upon the variety of these aims emphasises the importance of a school establishing clear priorities in aims pretty early on. For it would seem likely that otherwise those involved might have significantly different purposes in mind in supporting the programme. I suspect that several possible dangers could arise here, although there was little direct evidence from the study to support these fears.

Firstly, CSS staff might have unrealistic expectations as to the likely effects of CSS, and thus be disappointed by what are, in reality, significant albeit modest successes.

Secondly, accepting too wide a spread of aims might make the purpose of a programme too diffuse for either staff or pupils to have a real sense of direction or purpose in planning and assessing their collective progress, with a subsequent decline in morale on both sides.

Thirdly, practical decisions about programme structure, job and pupil selection and assessment methods must all bear some intelligible relationships to the aims of the programme. Otherwise a wide diversity of aims (or a lack of clarity about relative priorities amongst them) may lead to incompatible policies being adopted in relation to different aspects of the work that make the successful achievement of any of the aims (let alone all of them) much less likely.

Fourthly, a plausible match must be maintained between the stated aims of the programme and the scale of the resources requested to achieve them. While it was impossible to quantify the staffing demands of CSS precisely, it seemed that none of the schools visited was allocating more than 1—2 per cent of their timetable staffing time to CSS. To claim that staffing on this scale would simultaneously achieve all the aims mentioned earlier in this section would be liable to create justifiable scepticism amongst staff not directly involved with the work, particularly given the genuine difficulties involved in demonstrating success in anything more than an anecdotal way.

Finally, it is possible that a sense of unease amongst supporters of CSS about the practicability of achieving their ideals could lead them to an unconscious avoidance of careful and extensive evaluation of the results of their work.

Community service, then, is an activity which may be taken up for many reasons. In part, the particular form that a programme takes will depend upon the aims (both implicit and explicit) that those responsible for introducing the programme have in mind. But this is only one factor at work in determining the form that a specific programme takes in a school. The background and experience of the staff involved, the sort of pupils taking part in the programme and the amount of time available for it are some of the more obvious additional influences at work in generating differences between programmes.

Even within the three schools studied, differences were surprisingly wide. Between them, they offered six programmes with a community service element (the list is not exhaustive).

1 An extracurricular programme run by a teacher of Religious Studies, drawing its pupils largely from the Third Form.
2 A Fifth Year non-examination CSS option, run by a Community Tutor with a large service element supported by action-based studies of the needs of the local community.
3 A Fifth Year Community Service programme, run by a Community Tutor but linked with the school's Humanities course, and with the possibility of the pupil's community service work being written up into a report that could form part of a CSE examination.
4 A non-examined Fifth Year Child Development course taken by the School Counsellor that included some experience with small children as a practical element.

5 An examined Fifth Year course on Environmental Studies in which a tree planting project (organised by the Science teacher concerned) formed a practical demonstration of the way in which a study of the environment could lead to action to improve it.

6 A non-examined Fourth and Fifth Year Community Service option, linked with a single Humanities lesson per week. The single lesson was used to cover broad social, moral and religious issues as well as topics linked more closely with the community service aspects of the work.

If any considered judgments of CSS are to be made it is necessary to try to make a systematic identification of the underlying factors which, in various combinations, can generate such a diverse range of particular programmes. This may at first sight appear an unduly abstract approach, but unless these factors are separated out it is impossible to grasp the complexity of the practical curricular problems that face a school that is taking on CSS. Furthermore there is ample evidence from other curriculum project evaluations[1] that this understanding (at both LEA and school level) is a crucial element affecting the success of the innovation concerned.

The materials gathered for the report suggest that at least sixteen separate factors must be taken into account if we are to describe, and understand the reasons for, variations in the CSS programmes and their effects. These factors are listed in Table 1 and discussed in the remainder of this chapter. The practical relevance of the analysis is summarised in the comments that form the final part of the chapter.

Before commenting in detail on the separate factors listed in Table 1 it is worth emphasising that the effects of a given programme are related to the presence of particular combinations of factors, rather than to their effects considered individually. So, for instance, two programmes which employ very similar policies in relation to the selection of outside jobs for the pupils to do may meet quite different problems because of differences in pupil intake to the programmes. These differences in turn may be influenced by

methods of pupil selection, by the availability of an examination link for the programme, and so on and so on. Hence the complexity and variety of the programmes, for obviously a very large number of permutations of different factors are possible.

It is interesting to note that a programme whose features tend to fall largely into the left-hand side of the spectrum as laid out in the checklist will be one which approximates most closely to a conventional school subject. Conversely, one which is strongly 'right-handed' will be very different from what teachers, parents and pupils tend to expect of a school-based activity. Clearly this will affect the ease with which a given programme is accepted, and the sort of expectations people have as to what it will achieve.

However to get a fuller picture, we need to look at how the different elements interact with each other in detail. Some of these interactions are indicated below, the most significant being discussed further in later chapters.

The three methods of pupil intake shown were all present in the programmes studied. There was some evidence that the choice of method significantly affected some pupils' attitudes to CSS. Also, the criteria used to select pupils would be directly relevant to the likelihood of a programme achieving certain possible aims (for example, improving the school's relationships with the local community).

As far as staffing was concerned, there was near unanimity amongst staff interviewed that a tutor's personality mattered more than his or

Table 1: Analysis of the major variable factors relevant to CSS programmes

Factor		Range of variants		
Pupil intake	1	Specific pupils invited to take part	General invitation followed by vetting process	Open access to programme for all pupils interested
Staffing	2	Teachers only	Mixed team	Non-teachers (e.g. community tutors)
	3	Poor staffing ratio	Medium staffing ratio	Good staffing ratio
Jobs	4	Selected to match pupil's educational needs	Pupil and/or community needs	Community needs met ('service on demand' approach)
	5	Obtained by the school	Mixed sources	Obtained by outside agencies
	6	Work in institutional contexts only (e.g. hospitals)	Both contexts used	Work in non-institutional contexts (e.g. individual homes)
	7	Enquiry/interview emphasis	Social emphasis	Physical work emphasis
Aims of programme	8	Focus on pupil development aims	Mixed aims	Focus on non-pupil development aims (e.g. improving school/community relationships)
	9	Pupil's cognitive development central	Mixed set of pupil development aims	Pupil's social/emotional development central
Curriculum Organisation	10	Timetabled (compulsory)	Timetabled (optional)	Extracurricular
	11	Single timetabled period(s)	Double period(s)	Larger timetabled blocks
	12	Fully integrated into wider non-CSS course	Distinct component in wider non-CSS course	Freestanding CSS programme
	13	Seen as curriculum/academic responsibility in school	Seen as pastoral/conselling responsibility in school	Seen as a non-teacher responsibility (e.g. youth or community tutor)
	14	Study element predominant	Study/service elements given equal emphasis	Service element predominant
	15	Direct access to regular funding as of right	Access to funds only by special request	No funds provided
Assessment of pupil's achievements	16	By public exam in whole or part	Formal system for including CSS report in pupil's references	No formal system for assessing, recording or passing on pupils' achievements in CSS

her professional background. However, the fact that Community Tutors were paid from a different source than teachers meant that where the Community Tutor took pupils during the school day, this either freed teacher staffing time for other work, or created improved staffing ratios for non-CSS groups. Conversely, in a situation where staffing for Community Education within a local authority was being cut back, it could be that a programme that depended crucially upon the availability of a Community Tutor might be more vulnerable than one which did not. There was also some doubt about the propriety of Community Tutors taking on work that was clearly formal teaching (for example, preparing pupils for examinations). Here too, then, there could be a constraint upon the kind of way in which a programme might be developed. It is also possible (although the evidence for this was slight) that Community Tutors were better placed to gain the confidence of some pupils precisely because they were not seen as teachers.

The staffing ratio for the programmes was highly variable. A programme running well above the usual figure for schools (and thus again saving staff for deployment elsewhere) would have certain attractions for a school, but would also labour under some major educational disadvantages. Most of those staff asked (but not all) believed that a good staffing ratio was essential if jobs were to be properly set up, allocated, supervised and followed up.

Jobs (that is, the community service work itself) could, as the scheme indicates, be found in a number of ways. In some programmes they were selected specifically to fit in with the study element of the course, thus being directly related to the educational needs of the pupil. Other programmes were much more responsive to outside demands for help. As a result tutors on these programmes found it difficult to plan a study element that linked systematically with the variety and unpredictability of the sort of practical experience a given pupil might be getting at a particular point in the year. This seemed in some cases to be leading to a separation of the study and service elements in the minds of the pupils concerned.

In part this problem was linked with the methods by which the jobs were obtained. Given poor staffing it is difficult for tutors to find time to go out and obtain jobs of the precise kind that their preplanned programmes demanded. Where jobs were sent in by outside agencies (for example, Youth Action Cambridge, or local community groups) this sometimes raised an awkward dilemma for the school, particularly if they wished both to find jobs that fitted the programme and to be seen by the wider community as always willing to help in whatever way they could.

Sometimes too there were numerical mismatches between the availability of pupils and the jobs offered, leading to pupils having volunteered but there being no jobs available for them within easy reach, or to there being no suitable pupils available to meet a specific request.

The extent to which a school relied upon jobs in institutions was also important. Where staffing was limited considerable economies were possible if the pupils were sent in largish groups to a small number of institutions, rather than being scattered over a wide area. This economy related both to the setting up and the supervising of jobs, particularly the former, as visits to institutions can often be set up on a long term basis, by contrast with 'one-off' projects serving individuals. Again there may be a distinct increase in the predictability of the pupil's experiences in institutions, which would make it easier to link such work with school-based study.

The type of work done on the job was another relevant factor. It was my impression (although some tutors disputed this) that most of the jobs were seen in social (chatting to elderly people) or physical terms (chopping wood). Very little use appeared to be being made of the educational potential of the knowledge and experience that clients had, although in one case interviews with the elderly were being used in a History project on the First World War. This sort of enquiry/interview 'job' (provided it also involved social benefits to the pupil and client) could be a very productive possibility for further exploration. The educational value of purely physical work was not easily visible to the pupils, or indeed to staff, although in practice quite a lot of it appeared to be going on.

As far as aims are concerned, it is sufficient at this stage to say that where the pupil's development is given priority, then the selection of jobs needs to reflect this, and a total openness to requests for help may be incompatible with that priority. Again, the type of job and the nature of the study element will need to be deliberately selected in relation to the kind of development (for example, cognitive as against social or emotional) that is being emphasised in the programme. It is worth noting that pursuing cognitive objectives may place considerably greater restrictions upon the sort of experience that is suitable than social or emotional objectives do. Put crudely, a pupil can (for instance) gain self-confidence in a wide variety of social encounters, but learning about the development of small children or the problems of the elderly requires quite specific placements.

There were no compulsory CSS courses in the schools visited, although they do occur in other schools. However, both timetabled optional programmes and extracurricular programmes were found. There was some evidence that courses of the two types drew upon significantly different pupil populations, although the degree of difference is probably very variable, depending upon (amongst other things) the ethos and pupil intake of the school.

The timetable structure in a school had a major impact upon CSS. Even where jobs were close at hand, travelling time and the nature of the jobs themselves could make single or even double periods of little use, as both pupils and tutors sometimes emphasised.

In rural areas where transport was needed to get pupils to jobs the problem was greater still, especially where there were a series of dropping off and pick-up points to be visited. The seriousness of this difficulty is linked with the job selection policy in a school, 'service on demand' and individual rather than group placements of pupils creating greater requirements for travelling time. Also the type of job that could be tackled was affected by timetabling, some jobs needing collection and preparation of materials and so on, and cleaning-up time as well.

As well as large blocks of time for the 'jobs', a programme with a study element needs smaller periods for follow-up and discussion, preferably close to the job time. Alternatively, a complete half day (some pupils wanted a whole day) could be used for a study/service programme, but this probably requires very careful planning to be successful.

Where the CSS programme was a self-contained unit, particularly if it was very largely run by a single tutor, planning problems were relatively easy to handle. Again, where the visits were a minor element built into a wider course run by a single member of staff the educational integration of the visit element appeared to be fairly simple. The greatest problems seem to occur where the CSS programme is envisaged as a separate but linked component in a wider pattern of school-based courses. Here there was sometimes some suggestion of a lack of integration between the components. This could be exacerbated by having separate staff responsible for the different components and not allowing sufficient planning time to staff in calculating their individual contact time loads. Given the widespread polarisation in pupils' minds between 'school work' and 'jobs', the educational need for close and continuous liaison in such situations is self-evident.

How the school divided responsibilities between senior staff also emerged as an important influence on the programmes. If, for instance, a school has clearly distinguished between academic and pastoral roles for teachers and senior staff, CSS can fall somewhat awkwardly between the two. Where there is also a senior member of staff in charge of community links the situation is potentially even more complex. This is because a CSS programme has aims, methods and demands for resources and contacts that extend across all three of these areas of responsibility. This makes even more demands upon staff time for consultations and policy decisions where community service is built in to a variety of courses. A combination of teacher and community tutor staffing also adds a further complexity to planning here.

The balance between school-based study and outside work varied considerably from programme to programme. What constitutes an appropriate mix would seem to be variable, depending upon the aims of the programme. Where pupils are expected to develop some structured and generalisable understanding of people, social relationships and factors affecting the life of a community or institution, a planned and systematic study element seems essential. Conversely an emphasis upon emotional and character development may be best met by maximising the service element. Probably the most difficult programme to mount is one in which a roughly equal emphasis is given to both types of aims. This requires (for various reasons indicated above) a type of approach and course structure that is difficult to create and maintain within the conventional framework of secondary school organisation, unless all concerned are aware of the demands that CSS is making upon the school and of the need to relate these demands effectively to the school's overall educational policy and organisation.

One important example of this problem is provided by the question of funding for CSS. The importance of this was partially masked by the fact that the three Project schools had special funds made available to them for CSS by the Local Education Authority. But in a more typical situation it is clearly important for a school to decide whether CSS is, for funding purposes, a department (or Faculty sub-section) with automatic access to funds in the conventional way, or something which relies upon repeatedly making a special case for money to continue its work. A third possibility is that a school might consider that CSS should raise its own funds as part of its work. The choice of any one of these three methods of funding has obvious implications for the long term stability of programmes, makes differing demands upon the staff responsible and perhaps signals to staff and pupils alike different judgments by the school as to the nature and value of the work being done.

The question of pupil assessment was a topic on which there appeared to be a fair degree of disagreement and uncertainty amongst both pupils and staff. The method of assessing CSS work varied considerably, from formal coursework assessment as part of a CSE examination to the informal transmission of tutors' impressions to senior staff for reference purposes. As a later chapter will indicate, the presence or otherwise of a publically examined element in the course seems to have a major impact upon pupil recruitment for a programme. It is also obvious that the choice of assessment methods needs to be systematically linked with the sorts of objectives being pursued and with the study/service balance of the course.

Perhaps less obviously, there were also indications that both pupils and staff were rather ambivalent about any form of assessment, often because they took 'assessment' as necessarily meaning assessment by written examinations. Thus tutors and organisers would sometimes assert both that the work definitely had valuable effects on many of the pupils, and that these effects could not be assessed in any way. On further questioning it sometimes emerged that this apparent contradiction (that they were certain of its effects but appeared to be saying that they could offer no evidence for their convictions) rested upon an assumption that assessment had to be quantitative rather that qualitative. The tendency to make this assumption may itself have been part of a rather stereotyped polarisation between 'traditional' school subjects and CSS, in which the flexibility of modern assessment methods in the former was not always fully appreciated.

Looking at the overall picture provided by the study, it is clear that there is no single clear cut educational entity called 'CSS'. Instead there is a multiplicity of different kinds of programmes, varying one from another in a number of basic respects.

However, the extent of this variety is not sufficient to support the view sometimes expressed that all programmes are totally unique and distinctive, with the implication that therefore no general strategy for improving CSS can be found. Instead what we have here is a range of programmes with varying points of similarity and difference between any two particular instances. The nature of these variations is summarised (albeit crudely) in Table 1.

This analysis has several practical consequences that are relevant to teachers considering introducing CSS in their own school. Firstly, it highlights the difficulty of making any global assessment of the value of CSS. It is quite conceivable that the reader might reasonably decide that certain types of programme were of considerable value, while others were, at best,

no more than a harmless waste of time.

Secondly, it emphasises the range of factors upon which the success of any given programme will depend, and provides at least some indication of the scale and nature of the forward planning that schools need to undertake if they are to have a better than average chance of success.

Thirdly, it indicates that any support an LEA, teachers' centre, or other supporting institution might decide to give to CSS would need to be of a kind that fully recognised the wide variety of forms that successful programmes can take. A policy that involved (say) providing support only for one very specific sort of programme could quite easily do more harm than good, by implicity promoting an approach that would in practice be unsuited to the particular pattern of conditions obtaining in a given school. What is required is a strategy that allows individual schools to decide what they see as their own educational aims in taking up CSS, and then providing them with that form of support that will maximise their chances of creating or extending programmes to achieve those aims as effectively as possible.

References

1 See, for instance, accounts of the experiences of the Keele Integrated Studies Project (Shipman) and of the Humanities Curriculum Project (Humble and Simons).

CHAPTER III

WHO TAKES COMMUNITY STUDY/
SERVICE, AND WHY?

As we have seen, CSS courses vary considerably, and the types of pupil who take CSS are correspondingly varied. To start with, pupils doing it as an extracurricular activity may be very different from those taking it as a timetabled option.

> 'I think that the people who do it on the timetable do it specifically because they are not very academically minded. I mean I think they are deliberately being chosen to do it; they have been asked if they would like to do it because they would otherwise be helping the gardeners or something like that, because they are Fifth-Form, may be remedial or very low academic ability . . . the voluntary ones generally speaking are very nicely middle class and very well motivated, and they see this as some social commitment . . . they are very well adjusted and very able children usually, at school.'
>
> (Tutor)

This picture of the pupil taking CSS as a timetable option is widespread amongst teachers and to some extent the pupils themselves. To see if it was accurate, a comparison was made of the entire Fifth Forms of all three schools, to see if the pupils taking timetabled CSS options actually were the non-examination pupils.

To do this, the examination entrance lists for schools *A* and *B* were obtained, and each pupil was given a numerical grade, based on the numbers of CSE and GCE subjects he or she was entered for. This was arrived at by the admittedly crude device of counting a GCE entrance as 2, and a CSE as 1, a non-examination subject rating as 0. Then each of the two year groups was broken down into four sets, made up of the twenty-five per cent of pupils with the lowest examination entrance rating, the twenty-five per cent with the next lowest and so on. Then within each of these four sets (or quartiles) the number taking CSS was found. In the case of school *C* a similar procedure was used, but there it was only possible to obtain the figures for examination *passes*. Clearly then the figures obtained from the three schools are not directly comparable (suggesting, incidentally, an interesting topic for future research). Nevertheless, we can use the figures to obtain a very rough indication of the relationship between examination entries or passes in each school and the numbers of pupils taking CSS. The results are shown on Diagram 1.

Even allowing for the passes/entries point, the diagram strongly suggests that there are significant differences in the programme intake patterns in the three schools studied. The question is why this was so. In school *A* pupils had to choose whether or not to take a two-year Social Studies course in Year Four. Of those who chose this some subsequently took Fifth Year Community Service as one of the three sub-options within the course. As Diagram 1 shows, there was a strong tendency for the Social Studies option to be taken by pupils with low

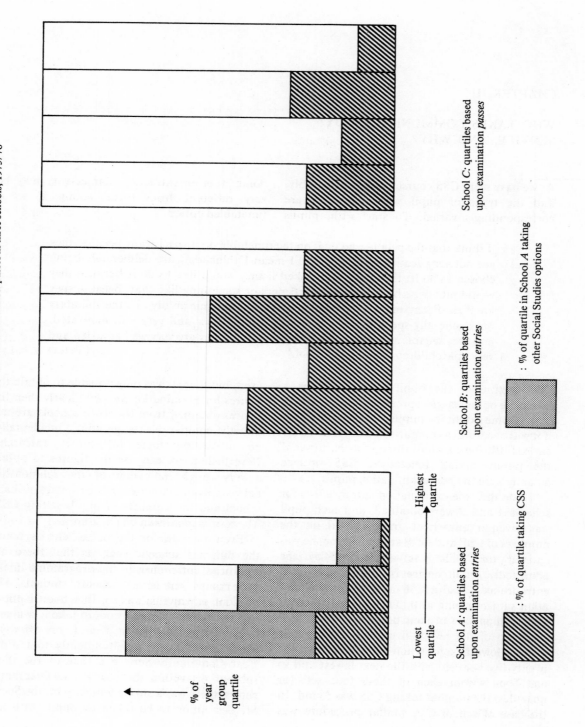

Diagram 1: Relationship between CSS and examination entrance/passes in three schools, 1975/76

exam ratings. No pupils in the top quartile chose this option, and only a small number in the next highest quartile. Within the Social Studies group as a whole, however, the Community Service sub-option gained its proportionate share of the pupils at each level. One teacher expressed a widely held view as to why this pattern had emerged.

> 'It's where it's placed in an option scheme. It's against French at the moment and most of the academic kids will take French, so those who opt to do Community Service will be by definition the less academic, the less able, the less intelligent kids.'
>
> (Senior teacher)

It is important to note that the figures do not fully bear out this view. In this school (as indeed in the other two) the genuinely non-examination pupil was a rarity; all the schools entered at least ninety per cent of their pupils for one or more examinations. Furthermore four out of five pupils in School A's Community Service group were in fact entered for some exams, and around half of them were taking four or more exam subjects. Thus although there was a definite tendency in School A for CSS pupils to be drawn from pupils taking fewer (or lower level) examinations, this was no more than a tendency.

When we turn to Schools B and C the inadequacy of the conventional stereotype is made strikingly clear. In these schools there is no evidence of any tendency for pupils with high examination ratings to avoid CSS. Indeed in School B there are slightly more pupils taking CSS in the top half of the year group than the bottom. Despite the similarity in the distributions in Schools B and C, the reasons for the two patterns appear to be very different.

In School B, CSS is very largely a visit-based programme, with only very limited classroom work linked directly to the visits. Thus it is a non-exam course, and we would expect it to be 'creamed' in the same way as occurred in School A. But in School B, Community Service is an option set against another non-examination course. As we see, when the curriculum is so organised that the pupils can take CSS without losing an examination subject, non-examined CSS was able (at least in this school) to hold its own in terms of popularity, with pupils of all the levels of ability represented in the school.

In School C, the situation was different again. Here there was a Social Studies course that could be taken either as a non-examination or as a CSE course. In both cases, Community Service was an element that could be included. Where pupils were entered for the CSE they could submit a short project on their Community Service work as part of their CSE assessment. So engaging in Community Service did not necessarily involve giving up an examination subject, but could instead be built into the examined part of a pupil's work. With this pattern too, we see that Community Service attracts a proportion of pupils from all four quartiles of the year group, with no evidence of 'creaming' taking place.

If these schools had contained a full cross-section of the ability range in their 1975/6 Fifth Years, we could thus conclude that CSS, if it does not conflict with examination success, is potentially an attractive subject across the whole ability range. But as explained in Chapter I, although the schools were in the process of becoming comprehensive, their 1975/6 Fifth Year groups were actually already 'creamed off' by local selective schools. Consequently these particular year groups contain only a small proportion of highly academic pupils (that is, pupils entered for six or more O Levels). Thus whether or not CSS would always attract its share of pupils from the highly academic group is impossible to judge from the evidence available from these schools.

While the diagrams tell us something of what the situation is, they tell us nothing directly about *why* it is so. To get some clues to this, we must use other evidence.

To start with, why was the School *A* pattern so different from those of the other two? As we have seen, it seems very probable that the setting of non-exam CSS against a major academic subject is what produces the difference. But why were they set against each other?

In School *A* the grouping of options was actually the result of a very extensive and determined attempt to find out what combinations of courses parents and pupils want, and then to design an option structure that enables as many pupils as possible to get all their preferred subjects. Consequently the fact that the option structure leads to the setting of CSS against an academic subject was largely due to pupil and parent preference patterns, not to the preference of the teachers. Furthermore there was very little evidence from the interviews with pupils of any attempt by teachers in School *A* to push pupils into one course or another. So it seems that the pressure that leads most of the more able pupils to prefer an exam subject to CSS in School *A* came (at least very largely) from either parents, pupils or both.

The views of parents on CSS could not be gathered directly with the resources available, but teachers and pupils made a number of references to parental attitudes to CSS. As virtually all the pupils interviewed were ones taking CSS there was little direct evidence to support the impression of a few teachers that parents sometimes discouraged pupils from giving up time to CSS, when academic work might suffer.

To get some information on this, one Fifth Year CSS group were asked what their parents felt about them doing CSS. The eighteen responses obtained divided into broad categories which are well illustrated by the quotations given below:

'Very good'	1
'A good idea', 'Think it's a good thing' etc.	6
'They don't mind', 'O.K.'	5
'I don't know'	1
'They think we should be doing exams', 'We don't work enough'	1
'They don't know'	4

Considering that these are pupils who have chosen to do CSS, this hardly suggests widespread enthusiasm for the work amongst parents a whole, at least in the school concerned. But perhaps the most striking thing is that four pupils hadn't even thought it necessary to tell their parents that they were doing CSS at all. While little can be deduced from such a small and informally conducted survey, it seems that probably here at least parents were generally seen by pupils either as not being particularly for or against the work, or as being in favour of CSS.

On the other hand, a few pupils interviewed had been fairly actively discouraged by their parents, but had taken the subject anyway. (One Fifth Year girl thought CSS very valuable as part of her personal development, did not think it appropriate to examine it, but observed with a certain wry realism that an examination qualification would have helped persuade her parents of the work's value!)

There was considerable evidence that concern about interference with examination work was a major factor in preventing some pupils doing CSS. Thus in the same survey of the Fifth Year CSS group mentioned above, several of the group believed that what deterred others was a wish not to miss lessons, or a need to concentrate on examination subjects. This reappeared in other groups too. Thus a group (largely Third Year girls) doing voluntary extracurricular Community Service were unanimous in saying that they would not take CSS in the Fifth Year, because of its interference with their other work.

Clearly then, where pupils see their schooling as centrally about passing examinations, CSS is at a serious disadvantage if it is thought of as conflicting with this pupose. The commitment of many teachers interviewed to an ideal of the school as encouraging both balanced intellectual, social and moral development was not getting across to many pupils, even amongst those who chose to do CSS. Even for some of these pupils, service to others and personal learning from that experience was a valuable thing, but not thought of as being an integral part of what schooling was about. As one Fifth Year boy put it:

'Well, I don't really see any point in it. O.K. It's helping the community but it's not helping our education. I think during the past year we could have done lessons rather than go out . . . It's not exactly helping with our exams, is it?'

The equation that that pupil (and others) made between education and passing exams is surely worth pondering on, even by those teachers who see education solely in terms' of developing a love of academic learning for its own sake.

Another claim that is often made is that CSS appeals largely to girls.[1] Here too the situation is far more complex than that suggests. In the three schools the Fifth Year groups taking more or less 'pure' CSS options divided by sex in very different proportions. Thus one group was almost exclusively made up of boys, while the others contained roughly three times as many girls as boys. To a large extent these variations could be traced to the structure of options within the schools, but other important influences were also at work.

It is generally recognised that some traditional courses are seen by many pupils, parents and perhaps teachers as sex specific — what we might call the 'metalwork for boys, cookery for girls' view. As CSS is a new subject, we might expect that it would not have any particular traditional associations of this sort. However there were some very limited but fascinating indications that such associations were in the process of being actively built up amongst the pupils in all three schools. Unfortunately the most striking evidence for this did not emerge until late in the investigation and it was impossible to follow it up properly. However the matter is of sufficient significance to warrant a speculative account of how the process appears to work.[2]

Firstly, pupils appear, the feminist movement notwithstanding, to have strongly differentiated concepts of what being male or female involves. However, these conceptions appear to be somewhat variable from school to school, quite possibly for reasons largely connected with the social mix in the catchment area rather than the influence of schools themselves. Secondly, these preconceptions influence pupils in their choice of some subjects, because the subject concerned is seen as requiring or developing 'single sex' qualities or competencies. Consequently these subjects recruit differentially from the sexes, and the preconceptions of lower year groups about the subject's suitability for boys and/or girls are thus further strengthened.

A new course label such as Community Service or CSS may not initially carry any particular single sex or mixed connotations for pupils. However, as this question of 'suitability' is an important one for many adolescents they presumably look for clues to help them find out if a new course is 'really' for boys, girls or both. Also, the staff may inadvertently make initial policy decisions which create a particular sex-image for CSS. Such decisions might include the following:

- Staffing the course exclusively with male or female staff, and/or with staff whose other work brings them more into contact with pupils of one sex rather than the other.
- Initially offering types of jobs that pupils consider only suitable for one sex.
- Timetabling the course against other options that pupils see as 'single sex', thus creating an initial imbalance in the first CSS intake.
- Coming to informal 'no poaching' arrangements with teachers of other options that lead in practice to imbalance, because staff concerned with the other option wish to keep a high proportion of pupils of one sex.

It should be noted that a staff may, of course, make decisions concerning such matters without any intention of producing an imbalance, but what seems to happen is that once such an imbalance emerges it may very easily become self-perpetuating for a variety of reasons.

Firstly, pupils who take a CSS course in the fifth year pass down information about it to younger pupils, including an assessment of its suitability for boys or girls. (In one school at least there was an informal but apparently highly active 'consumer guide' service for fourth years about the various Fifth Year options available. Information gained in this way was referred to by several pupils as a major influence in pupil decisions about whether to take CSS or not.) Secondly, once tutors realise they are in practice getting a largely single sex intake they may adjust to (or maintain) a pattern of jobs that reinforces this tendency. Thirdly, it is conceivable (although no evidence is available to support this) that CSS may become stereotyped in the minds of other staff and parents, as a 'girls only' or 'boys only' activity, and this may be conveyed to pupils.

In the three schools studied, such evidence as was available suggested that CSS had developed a definite image, at least for some pupils, that this image was often based on inaccurate or incomplete knowledge, and that it significantly affected which pupils chose to do CSS. But what was striking was the fact that CSS had a distinctly different image for the pupils in each school. Furthermore, whereas staff tended to emphasise the academic/non-academic aspect of the pupil intake, the pupils may well have been at least as much influenced by the male/female aspect.

In summary then, we can draw a number of tentative conclusions from the material discussed in this chapter. Firstly, which kind of pupils take CSS in a school is at least as much a function of option structures as of the particular features of the programme itself. Secondly, where taking CSS involves the loss of an examination subject, the CSS course is going to be heavily 'creamed', although it may still be far from having a totally 'non-examination' intake. On the other hand, where no such loss is involved CSS has the potential to recruit pupils evenly across a very wide ability range — a point which may be important for schools anxious to provide contexts for cooperation between pupils of differing levels of academic achievement. Thirdly, the early establishment of a particular 'image' for CSS within a school is likely to have long term effects upon subsequent recruiting for it, especially in relation to the balance between sexes, and possibly too in relation to its being seen as for low achieving pupils only. A school that wants to have a mixed ability, mixed sex CSS programme may need to devote considerable thought to how to achieve this from the start. However, there is nothing in the material collected to suggest that such a policy is impossible to realise. Provided a school is prepared to make the adjustments and preparations needed CSS can be not only nominally but also in reality 'available to all'.

References

1 See Ball, M. (1976) p. 13. (The number of school-based programmes covered in that study is not given but it appears to have been significantly more than in the Cambridgeshire study.)

2 It is interesting to note that in the nationally generated community service movement literature I have seen, the over-representation of lower achieving pupils in school is a frequent source of concern. There appears to be far less anxiety about the effects of 'one-sex-only' attitudes amongst pupils, although if these are very widespread they must effectively debar a very high proportion of pupils from community service programmes.

CHAPTER IV

SOME EFFECTS OF COMMUNITY
SERVICE

As Chapter II has shown, supporters of community service programmes saw them as having a variety of possible purposes. To judge a programme on its own terms would thus ideally have involved identifying the specific purposes behind the programme and then checking to see how far they were being met. Even this would not constitute a full evaluation of a programme. In the event lack of resources prevented the study even achieving the more restricted aim of a complete evaluation of the programmes on their own terms. However, some limited indications of the reactions of parents and members of the local community were found. These are discussed at the end of this chapter. More importantly, it was possible to gain a partial but illuminating picture of how some pupils at least reacted to their experience of CSS.[1]

Anonymous written replies to prespecified questions provided some of this information, but the major source was a series of interviews with individuals or groups (ranging in size from two to eight). All pupils were assured that their identities would not be revealed to anyone, and on this understanding all but one of the groups agreed to have their views tape-recorded. After each interview the group was asked if there was anything said that any of them wished me not to use. The only material lost in this way was a single comment on a senior member of staff. There was nothing that I could observe in the pupils' attitude to the interviews to suggest that their comments were anything other than an honest expression of their views.

This method of collecting material does not lend itself to accurate quantitative analysis, but on the other hand we can gain a vivid insight into the range of reactions to the programmes from the comments that were made. The main part of this chapter thus consists of a roughly representative set of extracts illustrating the range of views expressed, followed by short comments on each.

Extract One. Fifth Year Girl

I. Why did you choose Community Service?

S. I just felt that it was a responsibility. The school had given me a job and they thought I was suitable for it, and I was proud . . . We just felt we were needed and that was a nice feeling, you know.

I. Was it because the tutor said to you particularly that this would be a good thing for you to do?

S. Yes, that was what I liked about it. It was in the middle of a lesson and the tutor called my friend and I out and said she thought we were capable of the job and suited to it, and that really pleased us, because it wasn't 'All volunteers please come to the Staff Room', or something like that. We felt that the teachers had got to know our personalities and selected us, and that was very nice.

I. What have you learned from the work?

S. We learned that old people were just as interesting as young people. It was nice to know that some of the lonely ones thought you were nice to talk to. You were just a new friend. It was certainly worth doing from my point of view. I found out that I was much more patient with old people that I thought . . . I found myself at ease with them. I thought I'd be nervous, just being plonked with strangers, certainly not my age group. It was just fantastic — very enjoyable. It wasn't with the old people I felt nervous it was with the supervisors. One was very nice, but the others just looked down on you and thought 'We're just as capable as you'. Really we just relieved them, gave them a chance to have a cup of tea while we did the work. To us it was a privilege, but to them we were doing their work for them, so they did think it was a bit of a cheek I suppose.

I. What was it made you think they thought this?

S. Some would just bitch, and say 'Oh let me do that, I can do that'. And they gave us much simpler jobs. I don't know, it might just be my imagination but they didn't seem to like the idea of younger people getting involved with it, I suppose.
   When we started off we got the nicest jobs and they talked to us politely then all of a sudden it was 'Clean the floors' and 'Wash the dishes' — the jobs people were getting paid to do and they just sat back and let us do it . . . while they just laughed at us really, took us for granted. It was just sweeping and polishing and doing the housework, and we hardly saw any old people.

Comment

This illustrates clearly the educational importance of adults adopting the right attitude to the pupils. Here the pupil is initially given a sense of confidence and self respect by the tutor's trust in her, but this gain is then nearly lost through the reactions of some adult staff in the institution she is placed in. For many of the pupils interviewed one of the attractions of CSS was the implicit recognition of their ability to accept serious responsibilities, a recognition that they sometimes saw as sharply contrasting with the approach adopted by teachers in other subjects (see Extract Six below). The extract also demonstrates the way in which better staffing and follow-up opportunities in school could increase the value of the visits. The pupil (understandably) shows no real insight into what working permanently in such institutions might be like, and hence the reactions of the institution's permanent staff are just noted rather than being themselves made a subject for discussion and reflection.

Extract Two. Four Fifth Year Pupils (extracts taken from anonymous written responses)

Pupil A   I do it because I do not like any of the other options and I would like to think that I might have done something during my school life to help the community however small. So far in my life the community has always given and I would like to think I have given something back.

Pupil B   I do Community Service because I would miss out on orther lessons I do not like doing becaurse there is a lot of wrighing in the orther lessons and this is more interesting. And it would also mean I would be able to get out of school which I can not stand doing. (I hate school).

Pupil C   I was given a choice of this (Com. Service) or other options. I chose Com. Service because (a) I had already done one of the other subjects and wanted to try something different, (b) I did not fancy doing the other options. Those alone are not the only reasons. I chose to do Com. Service. Other reasons are that I think we should not always put ourselves first, other people should come first sometimes. That is I think one of the things this subject is meant to teach us. And it is easier to understand this by being taught this at school rather than have to learn it at home, by doing the occasional errand to the shops for the lady next door. Another thing that I think this subject teaches us is to do things and not expect a reward at the end of it. This is easily done under staff supervision, but it is not so easy when you are on your own, i.e. just coming back from doing a job for an old lady and when you get into the house she offers you payment for going and when you are on your own it is bloomin hard to turn down what she is offering you.

Pupil D   I like more manule sort of work to do in school. And I like helping people and the community so I can feel part of the community and not just a menice to society as I am sometimes referred to as. It gives me a chance to meet people and no what goes on in the communite. I get a lot of satisfaction be doing the work.

Comments

These four extracts raise numerous questions. All the pupils concerned were taking part in the same programme but, as the extracts show, their reactions to it were very different.

For Pupil *A* the main concern is to pay off what he sees as his debt to the community. Pupil *B*, by contrast, sees it as purely a way of avoiding 'school'. This kind of response (which although infrequent was not unique, or restricted to a single school) should perhaps dispel the myth that CSS will be an automatic success with the so-called ROSLA (raising of the school leaving age) pupil. However Pupil *D*'s reaction illustrates the way in which the programme, because it is so different from other kinds of school work, can enable some pupils to make a fresh start and to build up a different reputation and self-image from that which they currently have. How far the schools should go in consolidating such a change by public and formal recognition of pupils' achievements in CSS is an interesting question. There is an obvious risk that if staff and adults generally are seen as being dismissive of the value of community service then the pupils too will come to share this attitude (see Extract Five). Finally, Pupil C seems to have used the work not to alter his beliefs about what was right and wrong, but rather as an opportunity to develop with adult support, what he sees as morally good habits.

Extract Three. Three Fifth Year Boys

I. Why did you choose to do this sort of community service?

S. We were told we'd be in contact with people, like, and chatting. More often than not we're going out and washing the cars. We don't mind doing things to help them, like, but we'd been told we'd also be talking to them, and things like that.

I. How do you think the adult helpers in the handicapped club see you?

S. It depends on what sort of mood we're in really, because if we're a bit tired and that, we think they look on us as cheap labour, but generally they think of us as just, sort of, coming from school to see what things are like for handicapped people.

I. What is it about community service that makes you prefer it to the other option?

S. When you do the other option, it's a whole afternoon when you've got things already set down that you've got to do, and you've got a teacher nurse-maiding you everywhere you go, yet when you do this afternoon you don't know what you're going to do 'til you get there. You know basically what you are going to do but you know that anytime . . . you could easily walk out of school, we needn't even go there. We'd get into trouble for it, but the fact that you know you've got the freedom to go makes us want to.

S. And in the other option you don't get much choice, you just get pushed here to there all the while — they just tell you what you've got to do.

I. Why does the school run Community Service?

S. I think they do it because they want to get more pride for the school. So that the school will be more sort of posh — well not posh, but well known. They'd get more people to come to the school, more willing to come.
Some people go out and get us a bad reputation, so it (CSS) is just sort of

getting the reputation back.

S. The tutor told us that so far we've got a better reputation than any year before. Of course you don't know whether she's just saying that to kind of keep you going, or what.

S. It helps them out a bit. You see they've got a whole year to do the other option in that one afternoon, so they've got to spread it out a bit haven't they?

I. Why is it that in some schools there are mostly boys doing it, and in others mostly girls?

S. It varies from school to school, because in some schools the girls are more like boys, if you get what I mean, more tomboyish. And if you are a tomboy you don't really think about community service — 'oh, who wants to do that?' But like the boys in that school (i.e. one which had a majority of boys in the CSS group) might be, like, slightly femine, thinking like 'Well we think community service is a good thing'. They want to help people, but other boys, they think 'Funny — why do they want to do things like that for? They don't get paid for it'. It varies from school to school.
A couple of boys in particular in my lessons, each week they ask me 'What did you do this week?'. They want to know, they're getting interested in it, because their lessons are getting them down.
They think they'd like to do it because they think it's a good skive, but they think 'I can't do it because I've got to keep my face up with my mates. If I do that what are they going to think of me?'.

Comments

These three boys (as other parts of the interview reveal) enjoyed community service. The extracts included above are chosen to show some other aspects of their attitude to the work. The importance of being given responsibility for their own activities is again mentioned, and they also have definite ideas (rightly or wrongly) about why the school runs CSS. (In passing, they were the only group that showed any appreciation of the timetabling and staffing constraints upon a school's ability to mount particular courses.) The final comments are one of the three sources for the observations made in Chapter III about the significance of sex-typing in affecting whether pupils choose CSS or not. Note that boys (themselves doing CSS) do not question peer-group assumptions that wanting to help people is a 'femine' thing. It is also worth noticing that in that year group at least peer-group pressures amongst the boys were perceived as being strongly against taking CSS. How this belief had become established is not certain, but it is always possible that it did not originate entirely from the pupils.

Extract Four. Fifth Year Girl

I. Why did you decide to do Community Service?

S. Well really I'd never ever heard of Community Service . . . I didn't know what Community Service was about, so I went to see what it was like. What it really was meeting other people . . . we got shown round a couple of places and then decided if we would like to do a certain thing.

I. Having done it for a while now what do you think of it?

S. Oh it's great. I really look forward to that morning to be able to go. Only two of us go to this place, Blanksworth House (an Old People's Home). When we go there they know us now, we've been going long enough for them to know. It's surprising how they are neglected by the outside world. The only people they have (apart from the staff) are Denise and I to go. It really is good just talking to them and seeing how much pleasure they get just out of two schoolgirls going and talking to them.

I. Do you think you have learned anything yourself from going?

S. Oh yes, definitely, well just experience really. Before you'd say 'well anyone over fifty is an old fogey', you think, 'huh, the old . . . ' but when you get to know them and really get to talk to them they are really just lonely old people who have nothing in the world left (I'm sure their Mums and Dads must have died, you know), so all they are are just lonely. I've learned a lot. They're not just old fogies and you've learned how to cope. You feel that you're doing summat really worthwhile, you've got a real responsibility because you don't want to let these old people down. So you feel you are doing something good just by talking to them.

I. Have you learned anything about yourself from doing it?

S. Yes. I thought I was a hardfaced little thing who didn't really care about anybody (apart from myself) so when I went there I thought to myself 'ugh old people'. People will think 'she's looking after old people' and everything. But really I've learned I don't just think about myself and I do care about people like this. See, I've always dreaded getting old, I've always had this fear of getting old, not so much dying as getting old. And I just hope that when I have children that they won't just desert me. You really 'get into' them (the old people) and feel that you are one of them. It's depressing really to go, but you are bringing so much pleasure, just by spending a couple of hours with old people. I didn't think anyone would get pleasure out of me chatting away to them, but they really do.

I. Do you think other pupils . . . have got as much out of it?

S. I think a lot of them have got a lot of pleasure, as well as helping other people they've learned that life isn't just for normal people — well you can't say they're abnormal, but they are — they're not like us anyway. You've got to understand and have patience — you're not the only one in the world. It's not much to give up two hours to talk to them . . . it's not really misuse of time.

I. Do you think some people think it might be?

S. A lot of parents do, I feel. We had a talk the other week and the way some parents were talking, it was as if they thought: 'Oh my child should be at school learning something'.
Well, there's nothing like doing Life, is there? You can't experience Life in a classroom. Oh yes, it's probably the most valuable lesson I ever have — like, English is English, but whereas you're going out experiencing life as it is — well, not really experiencing Life, but getting to know other people. Oh yeah, I think the parents who feel it's a waste of time don't know it. Either their children have said it's a good old skive for three hours, or they don't really know what we do. It isn't made big enough; it's kept too quiet, what we do . . . And when the exams come, we stop anyway.

Comments

This pupil's response was the most striking evidence found for the educational value of CSS. It suggests not only a change in attitude towards the elderly but a distinct gain in self-knowledge and the beginnings of an attempt to grapple with the problem of what constitutes 'normality'. Starting from an assumption that being old is 'abnormal' and threatening, she has begun to revise her views, although clearly this process is still incomplete ('you can't say they're abnormal, but they are — they're not like us anyway').

The very widely held distinction between school experience and 'Life' reappears, but here too there are signs that she is starting to probe her assumptions about what 'Life' involves.

Extract Five. Group of Fifth Year Boys

I. Well, I wonder if I could ask you the kind of things you have been doing in community service work?

S. Well, I have been helping old ladies, and been doing gardening, and anything they sort of want doing. Painting, mending fences . . .

S. Mending the barn.

I. Oh yes, I saw the barn.

S. They wanted the impossibles done on that.

I. Yes, well it certainly looked a bit shaky when I came past. What about the rest of you? What have you been doing?

S. Well, we're working with just one old lady. It's all right, but sometimes it gets a bit boring when there's nothing to do. You sit around and chat. It's all right.

S. I'm with this same old lady, and well, we usually got something to do. The point is we don't have much time to do anything big.

I. Yes . . . what do you think she gets out of it, this particular lady? I mean do you think she likes you coming round?

S. Well, she can't do much gardening and heavy work, so we do it for her.

I. Yes, and do you think this is the kind of thing that makes it worth doing? I mean do you yourselves reckon it's been worth doing this kind of work, or would you rather do something else?

S. For some people, yes. Like Mrs Jackson over the road. I mean we just went over there to do fences for her. She couldn't have done those. Yet some people, like the barn people, they were young and they could have done it themselves. They don't want us really, because they could have done it. It's a waste of our time.

S. They were taking advantage of us. You find a few other people like that. Like they've got younger sons who can do their work. They just don't bother.

I. Yes, what do you reckon you get out of it yourselves?

S. Nothing really.

S. No, just the satisfaction of knowing you have helped somebody if they really need it.

I. Have you found out anything about the people you work with that's sort of surprised you?

S. I've known this old lady several years now. Before I even started on this work. There is nothing different really.

I. I've heard teachers in other schools say 'Well, it helps the kind of spirit of the school, and the atmosphere in the school, that you have got all these people going out and doing community work and it changes how the people in the community look at the school'. Do you think that is right?

S. No. It might change how the people look at the school.

S. If you can help somebody really a lot they think, 'Oh good, we can ask them next year'. They take it for granted sort of thing. But other people just think, 'Well, they've done it, they've done it, and they've gone'.

I. Yes.

S. No, I don't think it's a good idea. They think 'This is a good old school to get hold of' they think, 'We'll wangle round them'.

I. Do you think it makes any difference to the kind of atmosphere in the school?

S. No.

S. No one cares when you are not there.

S. The Head don't even know we are doing it.

I. Have you found this community service work, this kind of work where you are going out doing these visits, does it link up with anything else that you are doing in school at all, or do you see it as a separate thing?

S. A separate thing.

I. How do other people feel?

S. Well, I don't really see any point in it. O.K. It's helping the community but it's not helping our education. I think during the past year we could have done lessons rather than . . .

S. Yes, but you had a choice didn't you? . . .

S. Yes, you had a choice . . .

S. You could have done other subjects, anything.

S. Yes, but it's not exactly helping towards exams, is it?

I. How do you think other teachers see community service work?

S. They don't . . .

S. They couldn't care less whether we are in their lessons or not half the time, unless it's during course work sort of thing and the exams.

I. You think they feel differently about the exams?

S. Yes, they probably wouldn't let you go . . .

S. Yes, half of them don't go to lessons now, there ain't no point. I've never been to maths since after the exam.

S. . . . . . . (inaudible)

S. There's no point.

S. There's no point in cramming education for another week . . .

S. . . . don't care.

I. Yes.

S. I've only been to four lessons since I've been back. They don't really care whether I go or not. Like History, says to me and him the other week, 'Are you going?' and we says, 'No'.

S. He thought I'd left because I haven't been . . .

I. Do you think that the teachers actually, or some of the teachers aren't very interested in this work?

S. I don't think half the teachers know where we are or what we are doing.

S. There's only about three know what we're probably doing in the day . . .

I. Yes.

S. . . . nobody else takes any notice.

S. No. 'If we get rid of the trouble-makers in the school, we could get a bit of peace and quiet for two lessons.' That's what they most likely think. Not that I'm saying I'm a troublemaker.

Comments

This group was the most critical of those interviewed. Their comments (taped at the end of their fifth year, after the exams were over) suggest that at least some of them were generally cynical about both the school and the motives of many of the people they had been helping. For most of them both traditional schooling and community service appear largely to have failed. Whether their beliefs about the teachers' attitudes were actually correct is an open question (certainly they were quite mistaken in thinking that the Head did not know that they had been doing Community Service), but whether correct or not, their beliefs were visibly influencing their general attitudes and self esteem in a negative way. There is, of course, evidence from other research that schooling can help develop such attitudes,[2] so there is no reason to assume that their comments reflected inadequacies peculiar to the school concerned. Indeed my own observations would suggest that the staff there were more concerned than most to provide a valuable education for lower achieving pupils. The point is that here (as with Pupil *B* whose views are included on the written extracts) CSS did not automatically provide low-achieving pupils with the sort of educational benefits that its supporters often hoped for, at least partly because the pupils involved believe that it was generally seen by other staff as an expedient to get rid of them from 'proper' subjects.

Extract Six. Mixed Group of Eight Fifth Year Pupils

I. Why do people choose to do Community Service?

S. I think it's split up really, split into two, one side of the people choosing these things are genuine, they want to go out and they are interested in it . . .

I. Yes?

S. And the other half are out for a good skive . . .

I. Yes.

S. Anything to get out of work.

I. Yes. And what about the people who don't choose it?

S. They don't want to be interested in it. They are more concerned with themselves and what they want to do *or* there's not enough been told about it so they sort of said 'I don't know much about that so I'm going to do something else which I know about'.

S. Quite often most of them they're not sure what it is and they think it's visiting the mentally handicapped people and they're frightened, something like that.

S. Like when we went to Blankton, it frightened me because you know we're not used to it.

S. The first time as you go in to the Hospital you're a bit apprehensive but after we'd been for a couple of weeks we enjoyed it. You know, we saw it in a different light to that which everyone was telling how it was.

S. How terrible it was and we shouldn't go there.

S. It wasn't like that at all. People give it a bad name you know.

I. Are there any things in the programme that you have done that you think really expected too much of you? Not perhaps you, personally, but you know students generally?

S. Well, I thought I was expected to do a lot at the Hospital. You know they expected a lot if you were going there again. They were going to expect ever such a lot.

I. Yes.

S. We sort of forced ourselves to go really I suppose . . .

S. Don't know about forced . . .

S. Some of us were interested, some people weren't but when I took them along and after we really made an effort to get to know these people who were trapped in themselves and made an effort to approach them sort of thing, it really became easier and not quite so hard.

I. Yes.

S. They were terribly friendly anyway, the mentally handicapped children.

I. Yes.

S. So it isn't all that difficult really.

S. No, but trying to reach them in what they're doing . . .

S. Yes.

I. Were there any things in the programme that people felt were really too easy or you know they were just boring or not worth doing?

S. Visiting old people's homes.

S. Well . . .

S. Old people sitting all round the room.

S. Well, it wasn't that it was boring, it was because they were bored and . . .

S. They were bored which meant we went along and they had nothing much to talk about, they just sat there and we did the speaking.

S. They didn't do anything. All they could talk about was what they had had for breakfast, lunch and tea.

I. Yes.

S. That is the general conversation and what the weather is like.

S. It's depressing. It was such a depressing place, it pulled everyone down.

S. If only they could get something for the old people to do, that's what our general opinion was.

S. Yes, for old people to do, we could try and help them. Get a relationship going with a certain person and speak to them so that it is ever so interesting for them. They are just sitting around in a room, like we are now, just sitting in a room like this, with either a book or their knitting to do and the blokes, well, they don't have much to do.

S. The television . . .

S. Oh yes, they have a television.

S. It doesn't take long to get a relationship with one of them.

S. No, no it doesn't.

S. It gets them out of the art of conversation I think, just sitting there.

S. You know there was some people who were extremely nice to get on with and they could talk about anything but the majority were, you know, they just didn't have anything to talk about.

S. If they had something to do but a lot of them are deaf as well.

I. Yes.

S. If they had something to do . . .

S. Yes, but a lot of them didn't appreciate us going at first, they thought 'interfering kids' you know. They didn't really like it.

S. They're proud that's the thing.

S. They thought, some thought we were being nosey because they hadn't been told either . . .

S. Charity . . .

S. No.

I. Has anybody had embarrasing or difficult situations while you've been on visits?

S. Yes, there was something similar to that. One old lady was under the impression that she'd been brought there because it was a prison and they wouldn't let her out and I used to speak to her each week and suddenly she said to me 'Quick, ring up the police' and 'Come on, I'm going to take you to the 'phone box. Ring up the police' and she actually began to take me to the 'phone and she said 'Come on, you're kind, go and ring up the police and tell them'. So I sort of worked my way round — I sort of said 'Well, I'll go there tonight on the way home' and you couldn't very well turn round and say to her 'Well, no, it's not a prison' because she wouldn't accept it, you know. Very embarrassing.

I. I bet it was. Anybody else had any situations like that?

S. It was last week in the play group, this one little girl kept running up to me, sqeezing me and running away. She was doing that all day last Friday, all the period. So I got her, picked her up and said 'Look, I'm going to put you in the bin' and she started screaming, and she was screaming and so she ran off to her mother. It's embarrassing.

S. I went to a physically handicapped — to look after a physically handicapped little girl and she'd had a muscle disease that all her hands were clenched and when she was born everything was wrong and she's had operations to put it right but her mother had been with her since she was born all the time and whenever we wanted to take her out anywhere she used to scream blue murder all the time.

I. Why do you think that was?

S. Because she'd got used to her mother and wanted her mother.

I. Yes. Any other kind of cases like that or situations like that?

S. Yes. When we went to Blankton we went there once to just sort of, you know, and there was a lady sitting there on a chair in the hall. I went up to her and said 'Hello, are you all right? It's nice weather' and all that and she suddenly turned round and I thought she was going to hit me. She just flew and she started swearing at me to get away from her and leave her alone . . .

S. And 'you should be locked up' and all this business . . .

I. And what did you do?

S. She just turned her back on me like that and she went down the corridor and shouted at us and telling us we were all nuts . . .

I. And did you find that upsetting?

S. Yes, because it frightened me you know, because all I did was sit down and say 'Hello', try to make conversation and you don't think that someone will turn round and do that to you, you know.

I. Yes. What do you think staff in the school generally think about community service work? I don't mean the tutors and teachers who directly work with you on it you know, like Alan, but people generally.

S. We don't know.

S. The — they don't know much . . .

S. No-one talks about it. I don't think they know much about it, they don't get involved.

S. They don't seem to be concerned, they just say 'Oh, you're doing community service?' 'Yes' 'Oh, that's all right'.

S. It's just two words — community service.

S. I think they just accept it. It's one other subject — it's got nothing to do with them, they don't teach it.

S. It's just like a subject where you're supposed to be going out and you're not under control and some teachers don't agree with it and you're not allowed out — you might get up to anything.

I. Yes?

S. And you could do anything, sort of thing.

I. Well, they could be right of course.

S. They could be right, yes, but, well, if they don't sort of make a start and find out where we sort of go wrong, well, we don't get anywhere do we?

I. Part of this might be, you know, you might go up to a teacher and he says, 'What are you doing next?' and you say, 'I'm going to do mathematics' and if he's an art teacher he might say 'Oh well, mathematics, yes'. But that isn't what you mean is it? You don't just mean that they just think, 'Oh well, it's a different subject that I don't teach, so that's nothing to do with me'.

S. No. They sort of say, they think about it for a little while and sort of say, talk to themselves sort of thing, and 'Is it worth it?' sort of thing, you know. 'They could be doing more of my subject' sort of thing.

S. But they don't ever discuss it with us, to find out what it is.

S. They don't know if we benefit from it either.

I. But again, do you feel this is different from the case of an art teacher who never talks about how you get on in maths? You know an art teacher doesn't go up to you and say 'How are you getting on in maths? Are you getting something out of it?' You know he wouldn't think to would he? I imagine.

S. I know, but this isn't a subject.

S. This is a choice. This is voluntary.

S. Something everybody should get some knowledge of.

I. Yes.

S. Regardless of what . . .

S. Helps you cope with any problems that arise in your family or friends. Helps you cope with situations.

I. Why do you think everybody should have some knowledge of it?

S. Well, community service is *community* service. If everybody has some knowledge of what goes on in community service they can help to some degree in understanding other people's problems in some other social situation.

I. Sometimes I talk to teachers and they say 'Well, really this kind of work, I mean it's important that people know about other people's problems, and that kind of thing, but that's not the school's job. The school's job is to teach academic things, it's not to teach that'.

S. That's why some people say we shouldn't be let out, we should be shut in here all day, in school. We should be trapped in by a barrier sort of round the school. 'This is school, you stay here.'

I. When you go out on visits, do you think that on the whole people outside treat you as adults?

S. Some people do.

S. Yes, some people do.

S. Some people think we're on a skive from school, don't they?

S. Yes, they look down their noses and say 'They're school kids out from school on a skive'.

S. 'They've let us out' sort of thing.

S. Because a lot of them look when we go down the road with fags in our hand or something like that.

S. Perhaps we are but . . .

S. But that's not the point is it?

S. What we really need is a lot more publicity telling people exactly what we are doing because the majority of people don't know what we are doing. There ought to be posters or something or the other telling people just exactly who we are, what we're doing and what we're there for.

S. Yes.

S. Some people say 'Oh community service — that's looking after children and play groups isn't it?'.

S. No, it's not just that, we said.

S. No, but that's what they thought.

I. How would you like people to treat you when you go off on these visits?

S. As responsible people.

S. Who are willing to help.

S. Yes.

S. Well, it's someone they could naturally call on, call to in the school and say 'Look, well, I am going up to town or something and could you send someone round to look after my child?'.

I. Yes.

S. It's just another service or something that they can call on.

I. Yes.

S. Someone they can trust.

Comments

This group were very much in favour of CSS, and were anxious to see it given greater recognition. They were also constructively critical of the programme, but there was no evidence of resentment towards either the work or the school generally; indeed some of them were anxious that I should pass on their comments to the staff.

The interview suggests that the pupils (or some of them at least) gained in self-confidence and self-assurance from the work, that their involvement with the handicapped had dispelled many of their fears and prejudices about them, and that they had developed an increased sympathy for the elderly.

Here, as in other cases, being treated as responsible adults emerges as a central issue for the pupils, and is seen as something denied them in their ordinary school experience.

Finally the extract illustrates something of the potential value (and risk) of the experiences that pupils can have in this sort of programme. The embrrassing incidents described are all ones which could have been very productively taken up and used as a basis for school-based discussion with the group. However, comments made elsewhere in the interview suggested that such follow-ups were uncommon, although the group would have welcomed them. Other groups however saw their visits as so totally separate from their school experiences (even the study elements of the same programme) that they were visibly puzzled by my attempts to find out what they saw as the links between them.

No parents or clients were interviewed in connection with the study, but a little indirect information on their attitude to the work emerged. Perhaps the most important evidence for at least a fair level of satisfaction being gained by clients is that the pupils are still being accepted in institutions after a period of two years. I heard of no case where an institution had refused to allow visits to continue once they had started, although such cases might possibly have existed.

Individual clients, too were generally thought by staff and pupils to be appreciative; in one school I was shown some twenty letters of thanks, and told that others had also been received. One group of pupils mentioned people stopping to congratulate them on some repainting they were doing in a local play area, and so on.

The heads of the schools had somewhat differing experiences of the reactions of parents and the local community to the pupils' activities. One head described these reactions as follows:

I. What do you think people locally make of Community Service in the school?

H. By and large if they have experience of children who are doing it, either through being clients or through being parents, or through being people who are part of the Community Service support group . . . by and large these ones are in favour . . . The public around the school who don't come into direct contact with these children are generally against it, and would like the school to be much more concerned with examinations and preparing kids for jobs . . . I think this is related to our being a secondary modern school in transition to becoming a comprehensive. We haven't yet shown them that we can do this and get the examination results as well.

In the second school the head had received little direct reaction himself from either parents or other adults, although he believed that both positive and negative responses would be likely.

In the third school the CSS group's activities included a certain number directed specifically towards maintaining and improving relationships with people in the immediate neighbourhood. If, for instance, a local resident complained of litter being dropped by pupils, a CSS group went out to remove it. The head was sure that such activities (together with local awareness of the school's general concern to encourage community service) were beneficial not only directly to the pupils involved, but also to the school's reputation in the locality. Unlike the head whose views are quoted above, he had found parents reluctant to appear to be opposed to community service work, although some resisted the involvement of their own children in it, especially where such involvement was thought to be a distraction from their academic work.

Finally it is worth noting that some staff hoped that CSS programmes might have improved the general atmosphere and relationships within the school. This may have been occurring, but there was no evidence to support this hope. Indeed it is very hard to envisage a way of checking this, because to do so would involve separating out the effects of CSS in particular from effects created by everything else the school was doing. I would guess (and it is only a guess) that CSS can contribute to the creation of a certain kind of community spirit in a school, but only if this spirit is also being generated and maintained by a whole range of policies and attitudes amongst the staff as a whole. However, it is worth noting that some CSS activities (such as allowing older pupils to assist slow learners in the junior forms) may be particularly well suited to achieving an aim of this kind.

References

1 See Ball, M. (1976) pp.29—35 for further evidence on this matter.
2 See, for instance, Hargreaves (1967).

Part Two: Community Service and The Curriculum

CHAPTER V

SCHOOLING AND SOCIETY: THE CHANGING CONTEXT

It is a truism that modern industrial societies are in a permanent state of change, and it is another truism that schools both respond to and influence that change. Furthermore the way in which schools promote the social education of their pupils is likely to be particularly responsive to movements both in the wider society and to the general reactions of schools to such movements.

In the period since the early 1960s we can distinguish a number of broad social trends in Britain, some continuing throughout the period, others being more or less sharply checked by the decline in Britain's economic situation during the early 1970s.[1]

The sixties were a period of increasing opportunities for many people, especially for those who were young and male. There was increasing physical mobility connected with rising levels of availability of private transport, which extended the area within which individuals could realistically seek recreation and employment. There was greater social mobility, and for people coming to adulthood in that decade the chances of taking up occupations and ways of life different from those of their parents were on the increase. At the same time greater prosperity provided many (but by no means all) with the financial surplus needed to take up the wider range of choices becoming available.

It was also a decade of growth in the penetration of television into domestic life, providing an even wider range of vicarious experience and information upon which the young in particular could draw. In films and drama too, a wider range of ways of life was presented for general scrutiny, implicitly representing as problematic (or indeed outmoded) values and attitudes that had been taken for granted in the immediate post-war period.

For many communities, especially in the inner cities, it was a period of dislocation, dispersal and change. Large scale post-war programmes of slum clearance, and the creation of new estates on the outskirts of the large cities of Britain broke up patterns of social relationships that had structured the lives of many local communities since the nineteenth century. The movement of new waves of immigrants into the country, and their tendency to settle largely in the areas of cheaper housing also set in motion changes that are still continuing, including the creation of a yet wider range of life styles for the young of both host and immigrant communities.

The combined effects of all these developments included some that are of central importance to any view of the school's current role in social education.

Firstly, there was a steady erosion, especially amongst the young, of what for their elders were taken for granted assumptions about social, moral and political issues. To mention only the Campaign for Nuclear Disarmament, the increasing use of cannabis, the growth of new kinds of service organisations, such as Voluntary Service Overseas (started in the late 1950s) and 'the New Morality' gives some notion of the complexity of the changes that were taking place.

Secondly, there was a weakening of the degree of both control and support that the young received from traditional institutions. Wider opportunities for leisure and for working at a distance from home weakened the control of parents and the local neighbourhood over the young. Families themselves were increasingly being conceived of in more limited ways, with aunts, uncles and grandparents often becoming increasingly remote, both geographically and emotionally. At the same time the immediate family unit was itself more liable to disintegration, with rising rates of separation and divorce. Larger numbers of young people moved away to universities and colleges in their late teens, often from families which had no previous experience of what such moves entailed.

Thirdly, the notion of a distinctive youth culture came to prominence, imported (like much else during this period) from the United States. This crystallized and endorsed inter-generational differences, as well as feeding off them.

Thus by the early 1970s we may say that it had become usual to accept that there were greater opportunities for choice. Yet largely as a result of the same forces that had created these opportunities, there was less and less certainty within society about how these choices should best be made.

Beneath the surface of British society however, other trends were already beginning to make their presence felt, and as the seventies wore on, these became more prominent.

The economic base of productive industry in Britain continued to shrink, as traditional markets in the Commonwealth became more open to foreign penetration. The rising influence of countries such as Japan and the oil producers in the world's markets produced major external challenges to continued economic expansion in Britain, while membership of the EEC, together with the growing control of British industrial investment by multinational firms centered outside the country introduced a new range of problems and pressures.

The results of these changes in terms of growing unemployment and increasing divergences in the proposed political response to it are well known. The impact upon a society that had become used to increasing affluence was marked, forcing a major revision of individual and collective priorities, and increasing tensions between different social groups as a result.

This is, of course, a greatly oversimplified picture, but nevertheless it perhaps provides a broad background against which we may set the general effects upon the secondary school system of these changes as they developed.[2]

The first effect that comes to mind is inevitably the move towards replacing selective schools with comprehensives. Between 1960 and 1970 the percentage of secondary school pupils in comprehensives rose from under five per cent to over thirty per cent, and the percentage increased still further as the seventies wore on, with only the Conservative victory in 1979 preventing complete comprehensivisation of the public sector of schooling. (Private schools had, of course, never been strictly speaking selective in the grammar school sense anyway.)

The move towards comprehensives may itself be viewed as an important example of that partial crumbling of barriers that has been a characteristic of the last twenty years. Changing beliefs about the extent to which intelligence was a fixed quantity, objections to the claimed social divisiveness of selection and changing notions of what a commitment to equality in education entailed all played their part in making the move towards comprehensives acceptable. So too did the belief that it would be possible to fuel economic growth by drawing upon an ever larger 'pool of ability' to meet the rising demands made by industry for skilled manual and non-manual workers.

Two other policy decisions also made a major impact upon the development of secondary schools in this period. The first was the raising of the school leaving age, which retained in the schools large numbers of pupils who would have preferred not to be there. The second was the belief that a 'real' comprehensive would have to be a large one. As Benn and Simon[3] put it: 'The rationale behind reorganisation is that the single school of 1000 can provide three or four times the opportunities as [sic] two schools of 500'. These changes in the organisation and size of secondary schools and the nature of their pupil population inevitably raised new questions for the staff who worked in them.

There were questions about the sort of curriculum changes (both in content and method) that the raising of the school leaving age made both possible and desirable. Again, a variety of problems were thrown up by the increasing difficulty of keeping track of — let alone promoting — the social and personal development of individual pupils in larger schools with complex option patterns in the later years. The role of comprehensive schools in the life of their local communities was a matter of debate, especially given the growth in some areas of the policy of neighbourhood schools, and the anxieties of many parents about whether their children's chances would be adversely affected by the abolition of selection.

However in dealing with these potential problems the comprehensives also had certain advantages. A larger staff created more opportunities for specialisation by teachers, and made possible the creation of a number of new senior posts. Often there was also an opportunity to modify or extend the buildings and facilities available, so as to improve current work, or to provide quite new kinds of provision. The question facing each school as it went comprehensive was how these resources should be deployed to meet the challenges that the new situation presented.

How this question was answered varied considerably from place to place, depending upon local conditions, the educational beliefs of all those concerned and perhaps the point in time at which the change took place. No doubt in some respects schools and LEAs reorganising in the late sixties and early seventies learned from the experiences of the pioneers, and adjusted their approach accordingly. Whatever the reasons, by the end of the 1970s a wide range of concrete interpretations of what comprehensive schooling involved and how it should be conducted had already become established.

Nevertheless the broad pattern of external pressures described earlier in this chapter seem often to have been a major influence upon the general lines that development has taken in specific localities. The impact of these pressures upon the total curriculum of the schools is a topic beyond the scope of this book. But we can usefully look at the variety of ways in which approaches to the social education of pupils have been modified over the last two decades. Of course as with the changes described above, not all these modifications have been made in all schools, nor do they always take the same form. Nevertheless an impressionistic account can, I think, be offered that will be familiar to many secondary teachers, and will enable us to bring certain general issues into focus.

Pending the fuller discussion in Chapter VII, let us say that socially educated people can be defined as those who are characterised by the possession of a sound and detailed understanding of themselves and others, and also by their ability to behave in an intelligent and sensitive way in relation to others, both as individuals and as members of various social groups and collectivities. Even this admittedly general definition indicates something of the complexities that face a school in attempting work in this area.

To start with, it is obvious that a school's contribution to social education cannot be sensibly planned or evaluated in isolation from the rest of a pupil's experiences, past, present and future. For pupils come into the primary school (let alone secondary school) with a vast repertoire of social and moral beliefs, attitudes and inclinations. Furthermore, throughout their school career the social impact of family, peer group and the mass media interact in highly complex ways with the social learning that is taking place in school. Nor can we ignore (especially at the secondary stage) the question of the relationship between their current experiences and their adult life. These relationships include what they hope to become, what they ideally ought to become, and what in reality they are likely to become. These three are seldom identical and they must all impinge variously upon each other and upon what the school is trying to do for pupils.

The conclusion we can draw from this observation is that it cannot be the school's role to provide a complete social education for its pupils. Rather the school must be seen as making an important supplementary contribution within the total pattern of social development of the pupil. Ideally it does this by reinforcing what is good, countering what is bad, and providing any essential elements which are simply lacking from the pupil's experience outside school. But, as this way of putting it makes clear, the school's contribution cannot then be seen as morally or politically neutral. The social education that it provides (whether this is determined by choice or by chance), will inevitably be a force for educational good or harm.

It also follows that the question of what schools ought to be doing about social education is crucially affected by the nature of the current contributions being made by other groups affecting the child. If these contributions alter over time then what the school must provide is likely to need reconsideration. But, as was pointed out earlier, the last twenty years have been a period in which there have been considerable social changes outside the secondary schools, as well as a number of important organisational changes within them. These changes have of necessity led to a variety of new developments in approaches to social education in the schools, and it is to these developments that we must now turn.

As we have seen, the sixties and early seventies were a period in which traditional boundaries of many kinds were being partly or wholly eroded. This led to two partially incompatible demands being simultaneously made upon secondary schools. On the one hand they were required to take over an increasingly large share of what was traditionally conceived of as the pupil's social education, as other institutions such as the family, the churches, the local community and the mass media became progressively less reliable channels for the transmission of traditional values. To that extent schools were increasingly required by some to act as socially and morally conservative agencies, countering what was seen as the growing erosion of standards elsewhere. On the other hand the schools were also under pressure not only to adjust to the new ideals being promoted, but to act as standard bearers, leading and underwriting the movement for social and moral change that was taking place.

Given the vulnerability of schools to external pressure and the variety of commitments of teachers themselves it is hardly surprising that the result has been that social education in schools has evolved in a variety of ways, with changes being made that were often incompatible in their intended and actual effects upon pupils. During the period under discussion there has been widespread agreement that schools should be devoting more time and resources to promoting their pupils' sound social development. Sadly there has been an almost equally wide disagreement over what sound social development involves, and how it can best be attained.

The changes in approach to social education in schools have occurred in a variety of forms. Some have involved modifications within the subject-based curriculum structure that existed in the early sixties. Others have required changes in that structure itself, while others again have largely by-passed the framework of the formal curriculum altogether to create new kinds of relationships between pupils and adults both inside and outside the school itself.

Non-structural modifications in the curriculum content of social education have taken two main forms. The first has been to alter the emphasis or line of development of a 'traditional' (i.e. pre-1950) subject so as to introduce or increase content elements relevant to social education. In many schools this latter change has involved redefinitions of the scope of such subjects as English, History, Geography, Biology, Home Economics, Physical Education and Religious Education. The second main method of altering curriculum content has been to introduce (or in some cases reintroduce) additional subjects dealing with some aspect or other of social education. Examples here would be Moral Education, Sociology, Political Education, Health Education, Classics, Economics, Social Studies, Vocational Education and Community Studies. In between these two main forms have come a variety of hybrid developments involving the relabelling and partial-making-over of a traditional subject area. (In some schools Environmental Studies represents a transformation of this kind.)

In addition to modifications within a subject structured curriculum, there are now many schools which have reshaped the traditional structure itself. This modification may take the form of creating an integrated or inter-disciplinary area within what is otherwise still a subject-based structure. In a more radical form, structural change may involve the organisational regrouping of subject based departments into a smaller number of interdisciplinary faculties, with a concomitant strengthening of the tendency towards providing some interdisciplinary courses. Both of these changes may create opportunities for increasing (or decreasing) the social education elements within the whole curriculum, by provoking a wide-ranging reappraisal of the school's aims. However, social education is not only something which depends upon the pupil being presented with relevant content, although the importance of this should not be overlooked.

If, for instance, we wish to encourage such qualities as cooperative attitudes, respect for the views of others, or self-confidence, we must recognise that these things depend upon more than just the content of a curriculum. In order to develop them in pupils we need to look at how teaching and learning are conducted, as well as at what the specific content of that teaching and learning may be.[4] But it follows from this that certain aims of social education (especially those relating to qualities of character and attitudes) may be achieved by adopting teaching/learning methods of a suitable kind in curricular areas such as the natural sciences and maths, where the content being studied is, by and large, only indirectly relevant to social education. To this extent part of the rationale behind adopting enquiry or activity methods or replacing individual competition with cooperative group work may be the belief that such changes encourage desirable social attitudes or qualities in the pupil. If this is so, we might well look upon (say) Nuffield Science as being in part an innovation in both social and science education.

A somewhat similar point arises in connection with many of the changes taking place in social relationships within schools. The replacement, for instance, of a prefectorial system by one based upon elected members of year groups serving upon a School Council is an innovation in a school's social education work. So too are changes (whether official or unofficial) in the accepted pattern of relationships between pupils and teachers. Where schools or individual teachers encourage pupils to be on first name terms with staff there is (or should be) an educational purpose behind the change.

A more oblique but probably very significant change in recent years has been the rise of the school counsellor and the pastoral care team. In the early sixties pastoral care, counselling and academic teaching were very largely indifferentiated elements within every teacher's role. Since then an increasingly clear division of labour between pastoral and academic staff (and increasingly distinct promotion patterns) has emerged in many schools. Here too we see a major new force for some kinds of social education being introduced. This is especially so when the counsellor's role is extended from that of a person who deals with individual pupils on a need basis into a role involving timetabled contact with all pupils.

All of the elements discussed so far have involved innovations within the school itself. However a further development which may become of greater importance in the future is that many schools are now seeking to organise socially educative activities for pupils outside the school. Innovations in this area include such things as work experience schemes and local surveys and investigations of one kind or another. This use of the local neighbourhood as an educational resource is often linked with a change in teachers' role relationships, arising from an increasing willingness on their part to see other adults as educators with a special contribution to make to the pupil's social development. Thus much of the value of work experience schemes may be seen as lying not in the learning of vocational skills by the pupil, but

in the educative effects of the relationships thus established with adult workers. In a similar way inviting non-teachers into the school to talk to pupils may well in part be an element in the social education programme, whatever the particular content being discussed. A less obvious aspect of this innovation is the greater communication being established between parents and teachers. This too is often seen as a way of improving not only the academic performance of the pupil but as a means of improving the school's (and the parent's) effectiveness as a source of social education. Of necessity I have discussed these elements in innovations in social education largely as separate entities. However as the general analysis offered at the start of this chapter shows, to analyse them out in this way is not to deny the educational significance of the interrelationships between them. On the contrary, such an analysis gains most of its value from the fact that considering them separately enables us to reflect consciously upon (rather than merely sense intuitively) the ways in which they interact with each other in concrete school contexts. It is worth considering the recent history of successes and failures in innovations in the social education curricula in this connection. This history could, I believe, be very largely interpreted as indicating that innovators who failed to identify and respond to the relevant interrelationships between these elements were generally those whose innovations failed to fulfil their early promise.

References

1 For a readable account of these changes see Calvocoressi.
2 See Calvocoressi, Part 3, Chapter 3
3 Benn and Simon, p. 130
4 For summaries of research on various aspects of this matter, see Hargreaves (1972), Sugarman and Musgrave.

CHAPTER VI

AIMS AND OBJECTIVES

If the account given in Chapter V is even app-roximately accurate it goes a long way towards explaining the difficulties that face a school which is attempting to promote the systematic social development of its pupils. For in the absence of any coherent educational tradition in the area, schools are faced with a baffling task in interpreting and organising the diversity of materials that they are receiving.

If this is so, how should the schools proceed? In a later Chapter I will argue that we could benefit greatly from an organised national debate on this whole area, and from that it is to be hoped that we could move towards the creation of a soundly based tradition and methodology upon which individual schools and teachers might draw. But at the moment there is little sign of such a tradition emerging.

In the meantime (and for millions of pupils it is always the meantime that matters in curriculum development) it is within individual schools and LEAs that progress must be made. For if a national approach is as yet impossible, individual schools can at least set about establishing an internally shared and mutually intelligible conception of what needs to be done about social education, and how it is to be tackled.

In order to do this a major priority for the school must be the formulation of its aims in relation to social education. Where a traditional subject area is concerned, the formal statement of aims may not be necessary (or indeed desirable). But social education is clearly not an area of this sort. For within any school there will be a number of different staff groups whose teaching activities have a direct bearing upon the sort of social education the pupils receive. This means that there is a very real risk that nobody feels responsible for asking how far these different contributions are mutually supportive in their effects, or indeed how the various contributions are to be related together at all.

In such a situation one line of attack is to try to agree at least upon a shared definition of what social education involves, and upon a workable method of categorising specific objectives for social education across the whole curriculum. If this can be done it enables each member of staff to begin to see which aspects of social education his colleagues are concerned with. It may also highlight particular areas in which overall provision seems excessive, inadequate or indeed totally absent. The remainder of this chapter attempts to present one such categorisation and to show what contribution community service work might be able to make towards meeting some of the sorts of objectives suggested.

In developing this categorisation I have tried as far as possible to arrive at a formulation that could be used in conjunction with virtually any set of moral and political values to generate substantive aims. This is not to claim that any concrete programme of social education can be value-free, or to pretend that I do not have strong personal views about what such a programme should contain. But the presenta-tion and defence of these personal views is not the purpose of this book.

What then, in formal terms, can we say about the characteristics of a socially educated person?

As I put it in an earlier article,[1] such a person

'. . .must be able to employ an extensive social vocabulary in a coherent and sensitive way, if his perceptions of himself and others are to extend beyond a set of crude stereotypes, dominated by the very specific cultural context within which he has grown up. His understanding of this vocabulary, however, must not be merely verbal. A sensitive and coherent employment of it means, on the contrary, that it is firmly related to the human behaviour that he observes. Moreover, it is nonsense to assume that somehow the mere addition of terms to such a vocabulary will automatically generate an increasingly differentiated pattern of perceptions. To some extent the individual must already feel the inadequacy of his current vocabulary in the face of the distinctions he perceives. However, if these perceived distinctions are to be registered permanently and made the object of further reflections, then new verbal distinctions will have to be learned to achieve this. The process is best seen as one in which perception, vocabulary and reflection all extend and differentiate each other in a complex cycle of mutual interaction.

At base, such a process must begin with what is immediately perceived, but any large degree of descriptive and explanatory sophistication will necessitate the inclusion of theoretical, abstract, or general terms whose relationship to what is observed is indirect. Such terms gain their meaning from their relationship to more basic ones. Thus, while such phrases as 'the French Revolution', 'middle class values' and 'authority' must, in the end, be rooted in the world as the pupil perceives it, they are only so rooted through their links with a variety of other, more concrete expressions.

While the possession of a social vocabulary is basic to social understanding, it is not all that such understanding involves. Such a vocabulary enables the pupil to formulate beliefs but he must also have some conception of the considerable variety of ways in which the appropriateness of these beliefs, and their relevance to decision making, can be at least roughly evaluated, if not decisively established. This is no simple matter. Consider, for example, how some historical knowledge, a sociological theory, a religious belief, and a memory of some personal experience might all play a part in our consideration of a really serious moral dilemma. All could be genuinely relevant to the problem in hand, but the way in which we try to establish and balance their very different sorts of importance is highly complex.

This leads to what is frequently seen as a third component in social education, namely the consideration of value issues of a social, political and/or moral nature. On the whole I personally find it hard to justify any rigid distinction between factual and theoretical components of social understanding on the one hand, and evaluative ones on the other. Whether such a distinction should be made is itself highly controversial, but even if it is to be made, then we must certainly include consideration of value issues within the broad context of social education as a whole. A conception of social education which assumes that the pupil should be encouraged to see his role in relation to others as that of an intelligently verbose spectator is, to say the least of it, incomplete.

But even including the consideration of value issues within the area of social understanding does not provide a complete account of social education. The pupil must not only be able to understand social situations correctly and evaluate possible courses of action in relation to them. He must also possess the skills and personal qualities that will enable him to translate his decisions into practice. It is, after all, one thing to recognise what ought to be done, another thing to bring yourself to attempt it, and another thing again to attempt it successfully.'

If the reader accepts this as a broadly correct picture of what he takes a socially educated person to be, we must then ask what aims a curriculum policy would have if it were intended to contribute to providing such an education.

Three categories of general aims can, I believe, be identified which, if successfully pursued, would achieve this. They relate to the development of cognitive capacities, desirable attitudes and dispositions, and relevant skills as follows:

1 To develop an understanding and knowledge of the social (as distinct from from the mathematical, aesthetic, religious or physical scientific) aspects of human experience. This understanding should be of a kind that is demonstrated by pupils' ability:
   To describe, explain, evaluate and justify their evaluations of
   — the *crucial* aspects of the *significant* activities of
   — those *selected* groups or individuals
   — that it is *important* for them to understand.
2 To develop in pupils *desirable* attitudes and dispositions towards themselves and others that will incline them to want to act in *appropriate* ways in social situations of all kinds.
3 To enable pupils to develop the social skills *necessary* in order to make an intelligent attempt to act *as they should.*

While this classification is not totally value-free it is, I hope, a reasonably open one, which could be used by readers with very different political and moral views to analyse and order their substantive educational intentions in this area of the curriculum. To do this, the individual (or group) concerned needs to give specific content to the words and phrases italicized, in relation to the particular programme or programmes they are studying.

However, even considered as a more or less purely formal statement of aims, this present-ation has at least one serious deficiency. This concerns the groups and individuals to be

studied. On one level this is a substantive matter upon which I do not intend to comment. Whether the groups selected for study should be categorised in terms of, for instance, race, sex, social class, political or social viewpoints, psychological types, life-style, place or resi-dence, or whatever, is a problem that I happily leave with the reader. However there is one more general dimension that should, I think, be taken into account in any programme. This is a question of the balance that the programme's objectives indicate between a concern for individuals as such, and for groups of various sizes. The significance of this point may be illustrated by considering the difference in approach and potential educational impact of the three hypothetical history courses described below.

The first presents history as essentially a study of the biographies of specific individuals (whether chosen for their historical importance or as typical of a whole class of ordinary individuals). Here the wider social, economic and cultural framework within which they lived forms only a background to the immediate experience of the chosen individual. A second course, taking precisely the same historical period, might put its emphasis upon the life of a local community (perhaps that within which the school is situated). Here group psychology, and references to groups such as the local gentry or artisans might largely replace the study of named individuals. A third course, again dealing with the same period, might be cast in national or European terms, looking at socio-economic or cultural groups nationally, and the way in which decisions and events at such a level influenced the lives of the population.

Although the illustration refers to an historical approach, a similar point can be made (with greater or lesser force) where some other disciplines relevant to social education are under consideration. Thus in human geography, health education, social studies, or political education there is great scope for variation in the degree of relative emphasis given to the consideration of individuals or groups of varying sizes. On the other hand, some subjects or approaches to social education show an inherent tendency to make a concern with one or other level dominant. Thus a concern with individuals and small groups is a major feature of counselling, drama, the study of some kinds of naturalistic literature, and psychological approaches generally. Community studies, local studies and environmental studies may by contrast seek to draw the pupil's attention towards his membership of, and impact upon, a neighbourhood or city-wide grouping. European Studies, International Affairs, and Civics may be subjects that distribute the emphasis in other ways again.

This whole question of the balance chosen between individual and group emphases is important for at least three reasons. Firstly, if the emphasis falls at one point along the spectrum rather than another this has a complex but I suspect very significant effect upon the moral and political aspects of a pupil's development. A pupil who comes to see himself centrally as one individual relating to other individuals is going to be a different sort of person from one who sees himself predominantly as a member of his local community with his loyalties and interests centered largely around that self-concept. And both of these pupils are different again from one who comes to believe that his dominant allegiance is to a nationally or internationally conceived group based upon a racial, social or political classification. Of course, hardly anyone ever thinks of himself solely within one or other such framework, but my point is that there is considerable scope for different emphases here within a school's social education curriculum, and that these differences are morally and politically important.

Secondly, to aim to promote understanding of anything involves getting the pupil to see the way in which its component elements are (more or less harmoniously), interrelated. But to understand the activities of individuals involves understanding the small groups within which they live. To understand these in turn requires an explicit grasp of the ways in which they are affected by their relationships to larger groupings, and so on. Conversely, to understand large collectivities such as the European Community, the peoples of the Third World or the international proletariat requires that such collectivities are grasped as themselves covering many smaller groupings, varying from one to another in important ways. To understand what is common to Western Europeans involves also understanding what is different about the French, the Irish, the English and the Spanish.

Thirdly, it is at least arguable that nobody could be said to be socially educated unless they had some basic understanding of their own relationship to a range of collectivities to which they belong. To understand yourself involves seeing that you are part of (for example), a family, a local community, a society, a race, a social class, and a male or female person.

The upshot of all this is that when attempting to draw up a substantive set of aims for social education, those concerned need to consider two dimensions at least. Firstly, the substantive aims need to be formulated in terms of developing the pupil's understanding, emotions, dispositions and skills. Secondly, in each of these areas it must be made clear which individuals (including the pupil) or groups are to be the object of study in relation to each aim. If, for instance, we wish the pupil to develop an understanding of the problems of the elderly, it needs to be made clear whether we are thinking of an understanding of the specific problems of individuals, of particular groups (such as those living alone in the neighbourhood of the school) or of old people in Britain generally. For although an understanding of one of these categories is related to that of the others, these kinds of understanding are by no means equivalent, and would require significantly different methods of approach.

If this analysis is of value it would suggest that the substantive aims of any social education programme can be usefully organised by locating each of them within one or more of the cells in Diagram 2. Indeed if it is unclear which cell to locate a given aim in, then it is worth asking whether that aim is not itself less clear than it should be.

Diagram 2: A classification grid for aims in social education

Individuals and groups in relation to which competences are to be exercised

	Self	Other individuals 1	Small groups 2—10	Large groups 11—100	Large groups 101—1000	Small collectivities 1001—10,000	Large collectivities 10,001 +
Justify evaluations of activities of . . .							
Explain activities of . . .							
Evaluate activities of . . .							
Describe activities of . . .							
Have appropriate attitudes and dispositions towards . . .							
Have relevant social skills in relation to . . .							

Pupil competences to be developed

In forming the horizontal classifications I have used both rough descriptive labels and specific numbers to categorise groups and collectivities. Neither device is entirely satisfactory, because verbal labels (such as 'the community' or 'society') are often too ambiguous to be really practicable for curriculum planning. On the other hand, the use of exact numbers is too precise if interpreted pedantically. What I hope the classification will do though is to indicate that within any particular school's curriculum planning activities there is a need to tie down a verbal label like 'the neighbourhood' pretty specifically in some agreed way, if the work of different teachers is to be effectively combined in the pupil's total social education curriculum. Furthermore to give precise numerical definitions to the cells of the grid helps to show where there are gaps or potential overlaps in provision. This cannot be seen as easily if teachers are working with very vague aims such as 'developing interpersonal communication skills'.

Let us now turn our attention more specifically to the matter of objectives for community service programmes. Here I propose to concentrate exclusively upon the potential contribution such programmes may make to promoting the pupil's social education, for this is obviously the major reason that most schools have for taking on the activity. However two points must be borne in mind here. The first is that, as has been mentioned earlier, community service may legitimately be valued for its contribution to the achievement of purposes other than those directly connected with the education of the pupils involved. Secondly, it must not be assumed that the only educational objectives of a community service programme will necessarily be in the area of social education. For instance some programmes, (such as those involving the design and construction of equipment for the handicapped) may also have scientific or technological objectives. Indeed it is quite possible to envisage

such a programme being planned almost entirely in order to meet such objectives and to benefit the clients, with the social development of the pupil being a relatively minor consideration. It is worth remembering also that amongst the non-social objectives in such cases might be the development of (for instance) positive attitudes to science and technology in the pupil, by demonstrating very concretely the practical human benefits that these two disciplines can provide.

Nevertheless it is self-evident that for most teachers community service is an activity in which the social education of the pupils involved should be a major priority. What then can this activity be reasonably expected to offer in this area? Here it is important to distinguish between community service as an activity, and any school-based element of community stuidies that may be linked to it. Let us begin with community service in isolation.

When engaged in community service pupils are actively involved in attempting to provide a solution to some problem faced by another person or group of people. At first sight this appears to give a very wide range of possible activities. In practice (and often for very good reasons) the actual range is far smaller, for any problem given to the pupil must be one that:

— the teacher thinks the pupil can actually deal with,
— the teacher considers appropriate in other respects,
— the client is willing to see attempted by a young person.

The first of these conditions is one which (in a service-only programme) means that the pupil is only given problems in which it is assumed that he can pick up all the relevant information needed as he attempts the task. It also assumes that the nature of the problem and its solution can be given to him more or less ready made, for the programme includes little or no time for reflection on, or discussion of, alternative approaches.

Depending upon the teacher's assessment of the pupil's capacities, this can mean that the pupil is in practice only given tasks involving dealings with individuals or small face-to-face groups, for the necessary understanding of how to approach or deal with large groups or institutions cannot be assumed.

At the same time a service-only approach is likely to give minimal emphasis to the need to try to explain why the client's problem exists, or whether or not a given response to it is justifiable. There is rather a need for a speedy descriptive assessment of how things are, an intuitive evaluation by the pupil or (more commonly) the teacher of what needs doing, after which the pupil is required to buckle down to the task as it has been defined.

The second condition (that the teacher thinks the task appropriate as well as feasible) may well cut out a lot of apparent possibilities. The need for clients to seek (or at least to accept) the help of young people introduces no new constraints upon the type of task available, but means that those already described above are applied, if anything, even more tightly.

The effect of all this is to make a service-only programme one which is, generally speaking, only suited to achieving a certain range of social education objectives. Presented diagramatically in terms of the objectives grid given earlier, the central contribution of such a programme lies in the shaded area in Diagram 3.

Diagram 3: Social education aims for which 'service-only' programmes may be used.

Individuals and groups in relation to which competences are to be exercised

Pupil competences to be developed		Self	Other individuals 1	Small groups 2—10	Large groups 11—100	Large groups 101—1000	Small collectivities 1001—10,000	Large collectivities 10,001 +
	Justify evaluations of activities of . . .							
	Explain activities of . . .							
	Evaluate activities of . . .							
	Describe activities of . . .							
	Have appropriate attitudes and dispositions towards . . .		▨	▨				
	Have relevant social skills in relation to . . .		▨	▨				

As this mode of presentation makes clear, this potentially represents a real but limited contribution to an overall programme for social education. But if we think in terms of a programme involving both service and study elements (whether integrated or merely co-ordinated) then a number of further possibilities present themselves.

The first is that the additional classroom-based time might be used to improve the effectiveness with which the objectives of service-only programmes are pursued. This could involve systematic pre-visit briefings, post-visit reporting back sessions or ideally both. Such periods can improve effectiveness in various ways. Besides the obvious benefits of improved pre-visit information, follow-up sessions also provide opportunities for public recognition of the pupil's efforts, from both the teacher and other pupils. Such recognition can be both motivationally important and informative to pupils.

But the availability of a classroom-based time allocation also creates oportunities to pursue additional sets of objectives, in the area of social education. At the cost of some simplification, we can identify four general directions in which the range of social education objectives of a community service programme can be extended by adding classroom based study to it. These extensions (summarised in Diagram 4) are as follows:

1 Developing the pupils' self-knowledge, self-control and self-esteem.
2 Extending their understanding of the clients they work for by getting them to reflect upon why the clients are as they are, and how far their initial evaluations of the clients' situation are justified.
3 Reconsidering the immediate problems of the client in a wider community or institutional context, and seeing how this context affects (or even largely creates) the client's difficulties, and what changes might be needed at that level to improve things.
4 Developing appropriate attitudes and dispositions in pupils towards the local community in which they live.

Diagram 4: Directions in which aims of a community study/service programme might be extended.

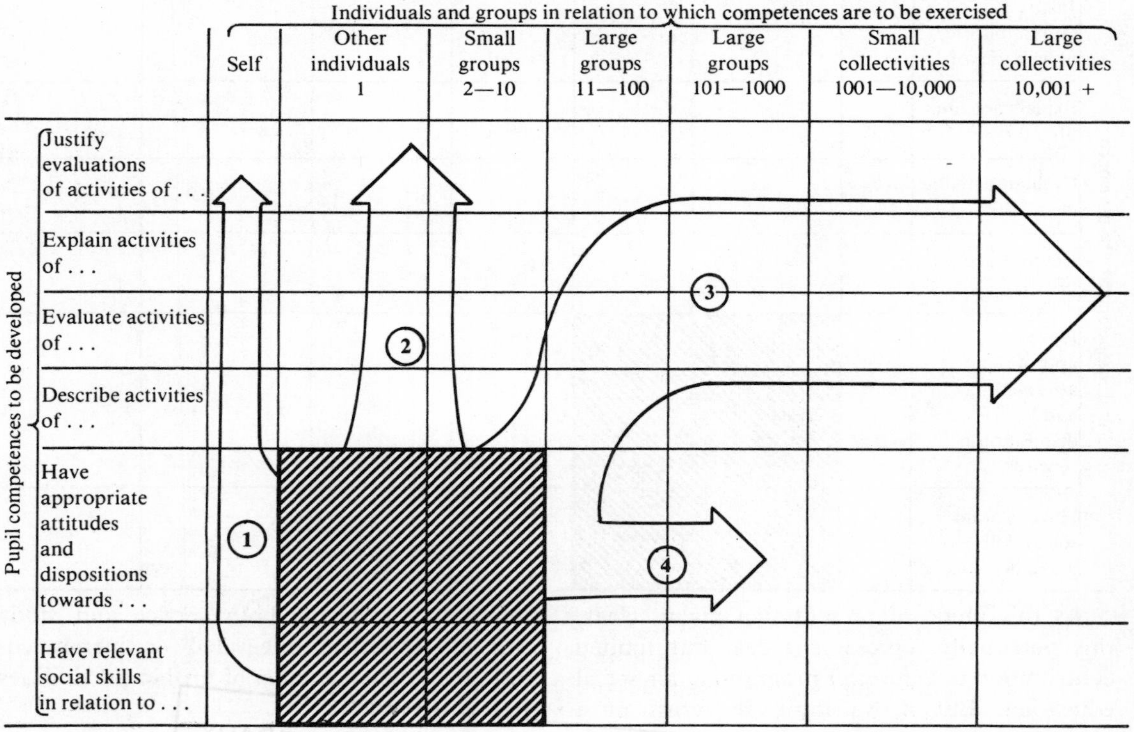

Naturally to point out that a community study/service programme might be concerned with any of these additional sets of objectives is not necessarily to suggest that a single programme should attempt to pursue all of them. Indeed it might be a criticism of some syllabi for community study/service courses that they would appear (on paper at least) to be too eclectic in their selection of aims.

This could be a matter of major practical importance particularly in relation to cognitive objectives, for it is very much easier, other things being equal, for pupils to integrate and absorb information, concepts and values forming an organic whole, rather than a disconnected set of elements having no thought-out inter-relationships between them. In this respect the grid might be a useful planning device for checking a set of objectives for their degree of interrelationship. Having said that, it should be emphasised that quite different principles of classifying objectives might be effectively used instead of those I have suggested, provided the classification had some sort of conceptual rationale.

The discussion of aims and objectives so far has necessarily been at a fairly abstract level, but the educational significance of the points being made can be illustrated by considering a concrete example. For this purpose consider the practice of sending pupils to dig an elderly person's garden. This is not only a very frequent task they are set, but also one which many teachers believe to have only limited educational value.

In a service-only programme, such a task can very easily slip into a limited educational format. The pupil is told where to go, hastily advised to try to have a chat with the client as well as carrying out the physical tasks involved, and is then dropped at the gate for the first session. If either pupil or client is too shy or anxious to get into conversation, the activity reduces itself to the exchange of a (temporarily) tidier garden for a cup of tea and an expression of thanks.

Suppose however there is a real opportunity to follow-up this activity in the school. What questions or issues might spring naturally from the pupil's initial experiences and interpretation of the situation? Once we consider this possibility seriously, numerous lines of development can be envisaged.

The actual structure of these lines of development is not easily represented in book format, for they are not neatly linear. Rather, they form a complex web of interlinked questions and possible answers that the pupil might progressively reflect on and discuss in school as the sequence of visits develops. But simplified into a linear format, they could easily include the points below and many others:

Q: Why can't this old lady deal with the garden herself?

A: Her physical limitations (leading to a consideration of these limitations as they affect the elderly more generally).

Q: But some people of her age can manage — why are there such differences in physical well-being amongst the elderly?

A: Considerations of environmental variations and personal life-styles, and their cumulative effects upon health.

Q: But even where an elderly person can physically manage such work, they sometimes lack the motivation to do it. Why?

A: Perhaps the garden was always her husband's responsibility (leading to questions about changing conceptions of what work is appropriate for men and women).

Q: Why doesn't she move to accommodation elsewhere which is not so difficult for her to maintain?

A: There may be a lack of alternatives at a financially realistic cost. (If so, why is this?)

She may have practical difficulties in selling her home anyway. (Leading to questions about council and national housing policies, the anxieties or lack of knowledge some elderly people have about estate agents, fear of strangers inspecting their homes and lack of confidence in their own ability to handle the complexities of moving.)

A: The available alternatives (say, an old people's home) may be unacceptable to her. (Leading to questions about why this is, and whether the old people's home is actually as it appears to her. This in turn can lead into evaluative discussion about what sort of provision should be made for the elderly, and what the practical difficulties of providing it might be.)

A: She may have a great personal attachment to the house itself. (This raises questions about why this should be so, and the importance to all of us, especially perhaps the lonely, of living in familiar situations, surrounded by familiar things, and by neighbours or children.)

Q: But if she has friends or relatives in the neighbourhood why don't they help with things like the garden?

A: Perhaps relatives and friends have moved away (if so, what reasons might there be?), or if they are still living locally they visit only infrequently. This raises speculations about how young people with their own families view their responsibilities to older relatives. Do they perhaps not have time to visit (if so, why?). Or do they try to limit their contact, and thus their responsibilities here? (This raises all sorts of further issues about family ties generally.) It also provides a point of departure for explaining the pupil's own reactions to the client. Do lonely people make too great a demand upon others because they are lonely, and so scare them away? Or are people now just more selfish? Why should it be necessary for schools to actually organise strangers (i.e. the pupils) to help the elderly? Are such visits actually a reasonable part of a pupil's education anyway?

I have laboured this illustration somewhat, but that is because it brings out in concrete form many of the issues this chapter raises.

Firstly it brings home the importance in planning a programme of a considered balancing of the pursuit of educational objectives as such against the desire simply to meet the expressed needs of a client or to improve the school's reputation. Clearly there is no need for pupils to reflect on all these issues if the essential point of their visit is just to show an elderly person that somebody is willing to help them with an immediate problem. On the other hand, the example illustrates how even the most apparently straightforward task provides real opportunities for pupils and teachers to achieve a great awareness and understanding of the human and social situation from which an ostensibly very simple problem takes the form that it does.

Secondly, it indicates the way in which an increased understanding can be gained by pursuing a variety of different lines of thought that the situation suggests. Some of the questions and possible answers lead the pupil towards greater self-awareness. Others begin to explore the psychological problems of the elderly and the lonely. Others again lead the pupil's attention outwards into the family and community context behind the immediate problem.

Thirdly it raises in an acute form the question about the relationship between developing the pupil's cognitive grasp of a social situation and increasing the sensitivity and appropriateness of his or her emotional responses to it. My own general position on this is no doubt clear enough from the line taken earlier in this chapter. On the whole, the more a person knows about the relevant aspects of a situation, the more likely I think it is that their feelings towards the people and issues involved will be desirable ones. On the other hand, a certain unease about this remains. The general problem here can be put thus: How can we present a human situation to pupils in such a way as to enable them both to refelect seriously upon the problems faced by

those they are intended to help, without simply turning the latter into depersonalised objects of study? Were an over-intellectual approach to have that effect then this would not only be morally objectionable, but also educationally unsound, affecting the pupil's emotional stance towards others for the worse rather than the better. No doubt here, as elsewhere, we need to try out approaches and see what happens, rather than jumping to hasty assumptions either way.

References

1 See Scrimshaw (1975).
2 It should be emphasised that the value of this particular way of classifying aims is something for readers to judge critically for themselves — the test is whether in particular cases it really is helpful in clarifying priorities and relationships between aims. For discussions of other ways of classifying aims and objectives see Wiseman and Pidgeon, and Tyler.

CHAPTER VII

THE COMMUNITY SERVICE MOVEMENT:
NATIONAL AND LOCAL DISSEMINATION

At this point we need to identify ways in which external institutions can encourage and support the dissemination of community service work as a curriculum innovation. To do this, let us first look at what forms the large scale dissemination of innovations can take, and see how far the spread of community service work in the 1960s and 1970s fitted into any of these patterns. Three basic models for the spreading of innovation have been suggested by Schon.[1]

The first (called the 'centre-periphery' model) assumes that the innovation is initially created at a single central point, and then distributed in a more or less complete form to those who are to use it. The responsibility for distributing the innovation and for both preparing and encouraging people to use it correctly rests with the central group who originated it.

The second (called the 'proliferation-of-centres' model) involves creating a number of secondary centres between the primary centre and the users. These secondary centres take on the main burden of supporting and encouraging correct use of the innovation at the periphery, while the primary centre in turn supports and monitors the work of the secondary centres. It will be noted that in both of these models it is assumed that the innovation cannot be effectively improved by users, only misused. Consequently the problem of successful innovation is seen as being one of simultaneously persuading users to accept the innovation while at the same time retaining ultimate control of the methods by which and purposes for which it is used at the centre.

These assumptions are not built into Schon's third model. This (which he calls the 'shifting-centres' model) involves assuming that once the innovation has appeared and been transmitted to other groups, these groups will modify or develop the innovation, then transmitting their own version of it to other centres. Thus a complex network of communication between different centres emerges, with different variants of the original innovation continually evolving and becoming more or less widely accepted from time to time. Rather than there being a periphery that learns from the centre there is a continually changing pattern of competing centres each learning from and teaching the others. Where this is taken as the appropriate model the problem becomes not how one centre can retain control over the others, but how the different centres can maintain open communications with each other. In addition, and most importantly, it raises the question (which the centralised models conceal) of what makes one version of the innovation better than another.

In their book *Education For a Change*[2] Colin and Mog Ball offer an account of the post-war development of community service work for young people. In their account we can trace a rough outline of the concrete development and dissemination of the concept of community service over some thirty years. This development is shown in Table 2.

This picture is markedly incomplete,[3] insofar as it applies to community service both in and out of schools. (The final entry on this table is a speculative addition of my own.) Nevertheless it is sufficient to substantiate the view that

Table 2: Approximate evolution and differentiation of the concept of community service

Approximate starting point	Form of community service	Sponsoring and/or support institution
Pre-fifties	Charity provision of money or goods for needy.	Victorian philanthropic tradition.
Late fifties	Full-time voluntary service overseas. Extracurricular or 'sports alternative' Voluntary service in local community (mainly private schools)	VSO (Alec Dickson) Individual schools
Early sixties	Full-time voluntary service in Britain. Voluntary community service for young people generally. Compulsory and optional timetabled community service for 'Newsom' pupils.	CSV (Alec Dickson) Task Force (Anthony Steen) Newsom Committee
Late sixties	Expansion for school-based and voluntary community service.	YVFF (Anthony Steen) Local authority sponsored organisations
Early seventies	Community service as basis for community development involving whole community. ?? Probable period of growth of 'studies-linked' community service in the curriculum, with examined CSS emerging as work seeped across whole ability range.	YVFF (Anthony Steen) ?? Individual schools (CSE Mode 3) ?? Local consortia of schools

community service as an innovation has been disseminated in a way broadly compatible with Schon's 'shifting-centres' model. However it also suggests that in one respect that model (as very briefly presented above) may be descriptively inadequate.

A reading of the literature that the movement has generated, together with the range of aims suggested for CSS by the Cambridgeshire group suggests that no one of the concepts of community service listed above is currently preeminent. In other words, Schon's picture of dominance in defining the innovation shifting from one centre to another may not actually apply. Obviously there has been a process of differentiation, with the creation of new definitions being the work of new organisations springing up after VSO was formed. But instead of earlier variants being eliminated by their rivals it is at least possible that they have, by and large, simply continued to co-exist with them. To check this properly would be a major undertaking, but perhaps there is some support for this speculation in the fact that in the late seventies most of the volunteer organisations that the Balls mention were still visibly in existence.

If there is a discrepancy here between model and reality it may help us to probe the reality more thoroughly by considering possible explanations. One such explanation is suggested in a recent book on curriculum innovation[4]. Dissemination through a pattern of shifting centres is, the authors argue:

'made possible by the technology of modern communication systems, which enable participants in the movement to have continuous access, via the media, the telephone and rapid transportation, to shifts of meaning and direction, and to maintain connectedness. Because the structure is loose, it is adaptive to these shifts, and flexible enough to regroup around the 'new'. Ad hoc leadership is by those who articulate the latest move, and cannot be maintained for long, because the leaders cannot control or monopolise the information on which counter-bids for leadership will be based. They don't have time to change the social network into an organisation (which might permit such control) before a new transformation occurs.'

In the case of the development of the concept of community education it is clear that some of the leading innovators (such as Dickson and Steen) actually did have time to transform social networks into organisations, and the nature of the innovation itself is such as to give such sponsoring organisations considerable influence over the form it takes within the area in which the organisation operates. To show why this is, let us look more carefully at quite what the innovation was that was being propogated.

On the face of it an innovation may be a physical entity (such as a minicomputer), a recommended procedure (such as mixed ability teaching) or a complex message incorporating factual claims, values and recommendations for action (such as that embodied in the Newsom Report).

But this sort of categorisation is too simple. Suppose we consider a prominent innovation in the sixties and seventies, namely the introduction of new audio-visual media into schools. On one level the innovation being offered here was a set of physical devices with a fairly clearly delimited range of possible uses. But for many supporters of their introduction it was not the devices themselves that aroused their enthusiasm, but rather the belief that in accepting these devices schools would be radically transformed in all sorts of indirect ways. Thus in analysing what he saw as the failure of this innovation in the USA, Hooper observes[5] that:

'It is an abiding irony of the newer media that despite their ability to revolutionise and upgrade the quality of education they can by the same token prolong and mirror what is already going on in school. Programmed instruction is a very useful and efficient way of dumping more information into children's heads. Computer-assisted instruction may actually *increase* the amount of drill and practice in the classroom. Closed-circuit television might be the worst thing to happen to colleges at a time of bursting student enrolments. Instead of the crisis forcing faculty and administration into retooling the whole system, television has made it possible to solve the problem of large classes in an age-old way. The lecture as *the* staple medium of college communication could now be set fair, thanks to television, for another hundred years . . .'

For Hooper, then, the success of the innovation was not to be judged simply by whether schools and colleges made use of the new media, but rather by whether in their use of them, they also committed themselves to the values and assumptions that educational technologists held. For it was the value of the devices as a means of promoting these values that had led many educational technologists themselves to value the new equipment in the first place.

It is arguable that the history of the dissemination of community service in schools indicates a similar ambiguity about what precisely the innovation was that was being promoted. On its most basic level, it involved no more than the proposal that young people should help others, with the official backing of the school. Viewed purely in these terms it may well have been a surprisingly successful innovation. Although no figures are available it seems that community service in one form or another was (and is) established in a sizeable percentage of schools. But for many of the supporters of community service in schools this was not the real point. What was crucial was who did community service, for whom, to what effect and for what reasons. Yet because the activity could be used for a variety of different (and sometimes downright incompatible) purposes, it was possible for variants of the innovation to emerge both within and beyond the movement itself, differing in the particular social and educational values that they embodied. It now becomes clear why the framework within which community service is organised is a major influence upon it. In the absence of any rigid limitations built into the nature of the innovation itself it is the organisation which directly decides who does what for whom (by its control over recruitment and the acceptance of job requests). Similarly it also at least partly influences the purpose behind the activity.

So far I have argued that the promotion of community service work by the various organisations involved (CSV, Task Force, etc.) can be broadly fitted into the outline of the shifting-centres model given earlier. However a further complexity is revealed when we ask who or what constituted the users in the case of this innovation.

In the early 'volunteer-only' phase the organisations already appeared to have a potentially ambiguous answer, namely that the 'user' was the individual volunteer and/or the individual client. Up to the early sixties an essentially voluntary concept of community service was differentiated to meet the perceived needs of different categories of volunteers (full-time/part-time, school age/post school age, private school/East Enders) and to mesh these with the perceived needs of various types of client (overseas/local community, handicapped/socially disadvantaged, individuals/whole communities, etc.).

But as the decade wore on a new set of influences began to bear upon the movement, created largely by its successful expansion in terms of recruiting new categories of young people and in making an increasingly visible contribution to serving different community groups in need. For both a result and a pre-condition of this expansion was that the movement's activities began to impinge directly upon the work of the schools and various other sections of the local government services. From that point on the further dissemination of community service and the values it had previously embodied was something that had to be conducted in a way that was acceptable to these other institutions, because the latter controlled, to varying degrees, access to many of the people and things which that further expansion demanded. Amongst these people and things were:

— new sources of recruits (e.g. 'timetabled' pupils)
— financial and other resources (e.g. premises and salaries for more community service organisers)
— additional clients (e.g. elderly and institutionalised people known to be in need by the social service workers of the authorities).

In the negotiation that this state of affairs required between the volunteer movement on the one hand and the schools in particular on the other, we appear at first sight to have a fairly standard situation that has faced many curriculum innovators seeking to introduce new ideas or methods into the schools.

However before discussing the effects of these negotiations upon the forms that community service work in schools came to take, it is necessary to look briefly at the routes by which curriculum innovations traditionally came into the school curriculum in the 1960s and 1970s. For this purpose it is useful to distinguish the schools themselves from what, for want of a better phrase, I will call the support and control system. By this I mean the loosely interrelated set of institutions and groups that together function to provide various forms of support for the schools while at the same time exercising a measure of direct or indirect control over them. This system includes the DES and LEAs, the universities, polytechnics and colleges of education, the national and local inspectorate, major private institutions such as the Nuffield Foundation, educational publishers, the teachers' unions, the teachers' centres and the examination boards.

Using this distinction we can identify three points from which innovations originate, and (with some degree of simplification) five main routes that they have taken before becoming established within the schools (Diagram 5).

Diagram 5: Innovation routes in the education system.

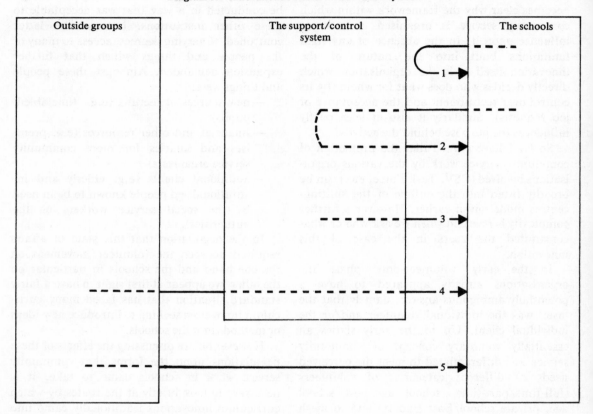

In summary these routes are as follows:

1   Small scale innovations spread directly from school to school without any substantial contact with elements in the support and control system at all.
2   Others originate in a number of schools, are fed into the support and control system and, after undergoing a variety of processes may or may not be fed back into other schools, possibly in a very different form.
3   Others again may very largely originate within the support and control system and then be fed directly into the schools.
4   A third point of origin may be some outside group which presents proposals to, or brings pressure to bear upon, the support and control systems to promote some change. The system then processes this demand

and, if it accepts its validity, modifies it in appropriate ways to produce an innovation that it then passes on to the schools.

5   Finally, an outside group may attempt to bypass the intervening system altogether and offer an innovation directly to the schools.

Probably very few innovations follow one of these routes in any simple way, and a number of intermediate patterns come easily to mind. Nevertheless this basic model brings out very clearly the fact that the support and control system can exert a number of influences upon the subsequent career of a particular innovation. This is because in relation to any innovation that passes through it the system may:

— endorse or criticise it
— authorise or (in some cases) block its movement into the schools
— provide or withold resources for its development and dissemination
— publicise or ignore it by controlling access to information networks leading into the schools
— suggest or require modifications in it
— provide or withold a range of expert advice on ways of improving the proposal and of increasing the likelihood of its acceptance by schools
— provide the training facilities necessary for teachers to implement the innovation effectively.

It would be a mistake to conclude from this catalogue that the support and control system is a monolithic entity which comes, so to speak, to a collective decision about a given development and then acts unanimously and efficiently to implement its decision. On the contrary, many of the difficulties faced by large scale innovations can be traced to the fact that the separate institutions within this system may differ in their judgement as to the value of a particular innovation. This is important because the different institutions also exert semi-independent powers over the various kinds of support,

all of which an innovating group may need to obtain in order to put its proposals effectively before the schools. Conversely, within the support and control system there are often a number of duplicate routes that innovators can use to reach their goals, and there have been some notable examples of curriculum proposals that were blocked by some sectors of the system finding their way out to the schools by others.[6] Nevertheless, given the scale of support that any nationally conceived programme of development involved, it was virtually inevitable that ambitious innovators (themselves almost invariably members of the education system in some capacity) would look to the system for their support. The community service movement has proved to be an exception (and possibly a unique exception) to this general rule.

As we have seen, in an organised form it was intitially developed outside the education system altogether, and it was only in the early sixties that it began to come into large scale contact with the education system. Furthermore this contact very largely took the form of direct contact with individual schools, by-passing the control and support system. This had the benefit of insulating it from the control and monitoring aspects of that system, but at the cost of also (generally speaking) foregoing the support that the system might have offered. To see in more detail the significance of this we must set community service within the general framework of the situation of developments in the humanities and social education areas of the curriculum in the 1960s.

The decade following the publication of the Newsom Report was one of dramatic growth in large scale innovation in the humanities/social education area. One writer[7] summarises a general view on the reasons for this growth thus:

'. . . in the 1960s the humanities moved into the limelight. This concern arose partly out of the Newsom Report of 1963 where the need to reform the curriculum for the average and below average pupil in the secondary schools was stressed. Up to 1960 history and geography, taught as separate subjects, were usually considered sufficient by themselves. But in the next decade these subjects broadened in scope and social studies in some form began to appear in the secondary schools. Social studies had for long cut across subject boundaries in the primary schools and now the integration of previously subject-bound areas of knowledge received support in the secondary sector.

This move towards more social and integrated studies was reinforced by the drawn-out debate over the raising of the school leaving age. There was unanimity over the need for a new curriculum for the young school leaver once the leaving age was sixteen. If that curriculum was to be interesting and useful it would have to be relevant to the lives of the pupils outside the schools. This was the educational context in which the Schools Council Integrated Studies Project was designed.'

It was also the context within which several other projects began. In 1965 the Farmington Trust set up a project on Moral Education. In 1967 the Schools Council (sometimes in conjunction with the Nuffield Foundation) funded the project on Integrated Studies mentioned above, together with projects on Social Education, Humanities and a second project on Moral Education. The following year Schools Council Working Paper No. 17 was published, presenting a case for timetabled community service work.

At the same time community service in schools showed every sign of further growth, with Task Force being able to report[8] in 1969 that they had involvements with 164 London schools, over a quarter of which had timetabled community service work. While there must be some reservations about what 'involvement' might mean in some cases, these figures suggest a surprisingly high level of dissemination.

Despite the apparently propitious situation that these facts suggest, no curriculum project based centrally upon community service emerged. The innovation route chosen by supporters of moral education (and later by those of health and political education) was not followed by the community service movement.

Instead the network of local volunteer groups continued to expand, apparently using the wide applicability of community service to negotiate particular area support arrangements with one or other branch of the relevant local authority. By 1977 the CVS could provide interested teachers with an address list[9] of 114 locally based young volunteer organisations.

These local centres were supported in a wide variety of ways, but insofar as their support came from local authorities, there is some evidence that it was usually the social services and youth and community sectors that provided it, rather than the school-focused sectors of the LEAs.

In addition to this network the movement also began to generate a range of published material. CSV has been a major source here (although by no means the only one). Their current stock (some of it dating from 1970) includes practical advice on how to organise community service in schools, short reports on a wide variety of programmes, specimen syllabi and lists of useful addresses. A considerable amount of topic-based resource material is also provided, including fact sheets, simulation games, worksheets and discussion notes.

Through the CSV packs, its local network

and access to such magazines as *Youth in Society,* the movement is also able to provide endorsements or criticisms of curriculum material originating elsewhere. Thus the CSV pack 'The School in Action' provides a list of some 50 books, magazines and directories with brief critical comments, together with a very much longer list of curriculum materials and relevant Schools Council publications.

These packs are linked with the CSV's advisory service, provided, as their introductory pamphlet puts it, 'to help teachers interested in developing school-based community service courses, and to develop new approaches to linking community service to the curriculum'.

The nature of the innovation route largely taken by the movement to date now begins to emerge. After having gained some degree of endorsement from the support and control system, the movement did not, on the whole, utilise the system to convey its innovation to the schools. Instead it adapted its own organisational network to provide local support for teachers or pupils wishing to carry the message into the schools. When difficulties arose in getting the innovation to 'take' successfully, the movement responded by generating what were perceived as appropriate materials and at least one central service to disseminate and develop the material. In short, where lack of access to the official system produced a visible problem, the movement simply created or adapted its own alternative structure to make good the deficiency.

However when we look at the alternative structure in this light, it is clear that its replication of elements from the 'official' control and support system is a highly selective one. A full study of the differences would reveal a great deal about the values and assumptions of both the educational world and the community service movement. However there is space here only to note that the movement has generated a system for supporting school work but is far less visibly concerned with *controlling* that work.

So by the late 1970s the volunteer movement had in effect produced (by a highly distinctive process of self-help) an organisation for disseminating their curricular message that was remarkably similar in some respects to those which a conventionally sponsored and funded project might have aimed at.

But what had happened when the movement's innovating proposals began to influence, and in turn to be influenced by, the schools? Statistically speaking we do not know, but there is enough anecdotal evidence from various sources to make it self-evident that a range of adaptations of the innovation emerged. On one level these variations may have been created by schools taking on the method and accepting some elements in the associated message but not others. Indeed given the internal variations already present within the overall innovation before it reached the schools that would have been almost inevitable.

But this cannot be the whole story, for in some respects the large scale move into the schools in the sixties and seventies apparently produced new variants of the innovation itself. In particular it seems to have prompted a significant evolution in assumptions about the range of young people for whom the work was suited, linked to changes in the conception of the purpose of the work.

Prior to the publication of the Newsom Report the range of young people the movement catered for had, as we have seen, already evolved to include both school and post-school age groups. The base in the schools, however, seems to have largely been in the private sector. The Newsom recommendations endorsed a major extension into the state schools, but at the same time by the very nature of its remit the report pointed to the lower achieving pupils as the new target group for the movement. Furthermore the overall drift of its references to community service was such as to direct the schools' attention towards the work's relevance to school self-help projects, to character formation and to its potential links with the meaningful employment of practical skills. By contrast the link with cognitive growth (let alone the possibility of a coordinated programme integrating cognitive, attitudinal and skills objectives) was very little explored. These facts, together with Newsom's visible reservations about the value of the soon-to-emerge CSE examination system, meant that community service was presented to schools within a quite definite framework, and with an equally definite pattern of emphasis. The message was that community service was best approached as a non-examinable character-forming activity for Newsom pupils linked to the traditional curriculum (if at all) largely through the practical (i.e. non-academic) subjects; a message essentially reinforced in Schools Council Working Paper No. 17, published five years later.

These two sources provided a formulation for the first solidly 'school-centred' conception of community service, But by the mid 1970s this recommendation was not the only one on offer to schools. A second approach to the matter was given its fullest embodiment in the book *Education for a Change* by Colin and Mog Ball referred to earlier and published in 1973. As the authors put it: [10]

'. . . our whole thesis is that our communities are disentegrating in the social sense precisely because it is unnatural for us to help one another. Time, therefore, that schools, instead of merely reflecting society, even protecting children from it, made service a natural activity. One of the ways this can be done is by making the whole school curriculum concerned with the needs and problems of the community and the individuals who comprise it. Every school subject and every school activity has something to contribute to this, and every school pupil must be affected. This last point is crucial. Maybe we have to live with examinations and the academic struggles that lead to them. That need not prevent this change. Making the curriculum relevant in every subject to community needs and problems is a prospect which will daunt the educational reformers of the Schools Council. But since Working Paper No. 17 nothing has happened. Time, we feel, that something did.'

There are several differences between this approach and that embodied in what we might call the 'Newsom' strategy. Obviously the target group of pupils has been extended to cover the full ability range. Equally obviously the target section of the curriculum into which the innovation should penetrate is also extended; all subjects are seen as providing opportunities for the work. What is somewhat less obvious from this extract (but educationally crucial) is that the Balls were also proposing a radical re-ordering of priorities in aims. Their thesis was not that relating subjects to the pupil's own social experiences through introducing a service element would help to make the subjects more interesting to pupils, (an argument which formed part of the rationale for the Newsom approach). They essentially argued for the far more fundamental claim that virtually the only rationale for inclusion of an activity in the curriculum was its relevance to revitalising the sense of community in our society. This they certainly saw as involving the development of knowledge and skills in schools, but in selecting which knowledge and skills to develop the central test was their relevance to creating and sustaining attitudes of community and compassion in pupils, and their value in enabling them to translate these attitudes into effective practical action.

Each of the two approaches so far described can be located within wider movements in

British curriculum thought and practice of considerable educational, social and political importance. On the one hand there were those who supported some kind of dual curriculum, with (very broadly speaking) academic learning reserved for the higher achieving pupils and attitudinal and skills development forming the core curriculum aims for the lower achievers.[11] The Newsom strategy tacitly takes up this curricular stance. On the other hand, some supporters of what we might call the community curriculum[12] were advocating a curriculum in which social education played a central role for all pupils. These wider ramifications cannot be pursued further here, except to note that the two possibilities mentioned are not by any means the only basic options open to schools in the 1980s in formulating their strategy for the whole curriculum.[13]

The Balls' proposals had been published in the Penguin Education Special series, along with books by such radical educationists as Illich, Freire, Reimer and Goodman. Thus unlike CSV (which publishes its own material)

they had made use of part of the educational support and control system to transmit their message. Nevertheless Penguin Education Specials were very far from embodying the central values and assumptions of that system.

A year after the Balls' work had appeared a book endorsing a third approach to school-based community service was published. This however originated from deep within the system, being the report[14] of the Schools Council Social Education Project. The project carried out a four-school programme of curriculum development involving, as a major element, a programme for community study to be followed by appropriate action. Quite a complex evaluation of the programme's effects was also mounted. The project team collectively and individually[15] went to some pains to distinguish their work from community service, but in reality some of their major concerns fell well within the range of aims that different supporters of school-based community service by this time advocated. The project team summarised[16] their stance thus:

'Social education implies a philosophy of education which lays stress upon certain propositions:

1   The proper teacher-pupil relationship is for the teacher to be adviser and experienced colleague and not mere dispenser of knowledge or arbiter of values.

2   The school's reward system and mode of grouping children must not emphasise failure or competition. It should rest on cooperative work among individuals and groups whose satisfaction lies not in obtaining points or praise, but in recognition by themselves and their peers that they have contributed to the task in hand.

3   An inquiry-based curriculum with individual and group research will sometimes result in action to change situations in school and community.

4   The school and community are integrally linked. The class is involved in the task of identifying ways in which school can be a supportive agency for change in the community.'

The basic similarity to the Balls' position is made even clearer by the team's further assertion[17] that:
'The basic principle of social education — that

everyone needs to develop the skills to examine, challenge and control his immediate situation in school and community—is a principle that ought to be applied in every school in the country, and for the children of all (so-called) levels of ability.'

Where their approach differed was in their implicit rejection of the 'social-education-across-the-curriculum' strategy of the Balls. Their programmes instead involved working with small teams of teachers who aimed to link studies by the pupils of their own class, their school, and their community with experience of active participation in formulating and developing the studies, and in some cases with community action projects. Thus although a number of teachers were involved in each school the impression one gains from the report (perhaps mistakenly) is that the programme itself was generally organised as a largely self-contained curriculum entity, although taking timetable time and staff from a number of subject departments. Whether this interpretation is correct or not, I will subsequently for convenience sake, take the Social Education Project as an exemplar of this 'free-standing subject' approach to CSS.

At the time of writing, community service, together with a complete support system has become widely established in schools. However it is already an innovation that has taken on a wide range of concrete manifestations, rather than remaining a unitary development. Even with the more conventional situation where curriculum innovations emanated from strong nationally established project teams this process of contextual variation has been widely noted[18].

In this case, as we have seen, virtually everything about the innovation's history to date has made the development of such variation almost inevitable, quite independently of the differences generated by the innovation's installation in schools of very different kinds. It is to the processes involved in that installation that we must now turn.

References

1 See Schon
2 See Ball, C. and Ball, M.
3 For a rather fuller picture, see Ball, C. (1977)
4 MacDonald and Walker, p. 18
5 Hooper, p. 413
6 See for instance Stenhouse pp. 127—30 on the genesis of the SSRC and Gulbenkian Foundation project on teaching and race relations.
7 See Shipman, p. 1
8 See Ball, C. and Ball, M.
9 See Griffith and Moffat
10 See Ball, C. and Ball, M., p. 33
11 See Bantock
12 See Merson and Campbell
13 See Scrimshaw (1976)
14 See Rennie, Lunzer and Williams
15 See Rennie
16 Rennie et al., p. 111
17 Rennie et al., p. 119
18 See MacDonald and Walker

CHAPTER VIII

COMMUNITY STUDY/SERVICE AS A SCHOOL-LEVEL INNOVATION

The Concise Oxford Dictionary provides two definitions of the verb 'to innovate'; namely 'to make changes' or 'to bring in novelties'. The ambiguous tone of the latter definition usefully reminds us that innovation (despite the natural assumptions of curriculum theorists) is not necessarily a good thing. Perhaps too it is worth noting that to bring in novelties is not automatically going to produce much by way of significant change.

More importantly, these definitions also emphasize the fact that schools are in reality engaged in continuous innovation, because a certain minimum level of intentional adjustment and development of curricula is an inevitable feature of ordinary school life. Innovation is not the sole perogative of highly publicized national projects, nor of widely known progressive schools. Having said that, both the level and type of innovation that a school takes on can be highly variable. The factors which create this variability, and their relevance to the task of introducing community service programmes to schools form the subject of this chapter.

In the discussion that follows some use is made of the notion of resistance as one barrier to innovation. In presenting the issue as one involving ways of identifying and avoiding resistance to innovation I am emphatically not assuming that such resistance is necessarily ill-conceived or undesirable. Whether introducing a particular change in a specific school is desirable is, in my view, almost always very hard to judge from a distance. Consequently whether or not the change should be resisted or not is equally problematic. This chapter is concerned in part with identifying the basic forms that such resistances may take, and some of the strategies that innovators may take to avoid them. If the discussion helps both supporters and opponents of a given change to understand the mechanics of change more clearly, then it will have served its purpose.

In the previous chapter some reference has been made to the external forces affecting which innovations succeed in (so to speak) reaching the school gates. Although the total professional autonomy of schools is something of a myth, the fact remains that members of a school staff have (collectively and individually) considerable influence over which curriculum changes the school accepts, and also over the precise form in which they are accepted. Traditionally the head has occupied a crucial role in such decisions, at least in areas where the proposed change requires no more than an internal change in a department's policies, with no resource implications beyond it. Although this influence is still considerable, there are some signs of movement towards a more widely shared control over policy in this area[1]. However no matter how widely this power is dispersed amongst staff (especially senior staff), one group that will have a special influence over the final decision are those who actually have to implement the change and live with the results. So any major innovation must be acceptable both to the potential teacher innovators themselves and, to varying degrees, to all staff (especially to senior teachers and other 'opinion leaders').

On the basis of their study[2] of the ways in which secondary schools react to major innovations, two writers have come to the tentative conclusion that large scale acceptance of an innovation depends upon teachers seeing it as:

1 offering solutions tailored to the less able adolescent,

2 based on a 'realistic' view of the limitations of the pupil,

3 respecting their 'autonomy' with regard to classroom practice,

4 offering reinforcement to their professional identities.

If this picture is correct, it provides some hints as to the reasons that staff might have for rejecting one or more of the three approaches to school-based community service identified in the last chapter (pp 63 to 66). Only the Newsom version offers community service as a proposal fitted especially to the needs of the less able pupil. All three versions take an optimistic view of the pupils' capacity to work without supervision outside school in what may be emotionally taxing situations, particularly if it is younger pupils who are being involved. All three can require some modification of a teacher's normal classroom practice (especially the Social Education Project variant) if follow-up discussions lead into areas of personal response or sensitivity that the teacher feels are beyond his province. Finally all three, especially the Social Education Project variant and that proposed by the Balls, call into question the conventional view of the professional role of the teacher.

In summary, what this indicates is that CSS will only be acceptable to certain teachers — and probably they form a minority in many schools. Consequently it can only be successful on a long term basis in schools in which such teachers form at least a sufficiently influential group to enable them to support and sustain the innovation against a fair degree of scepticism or indifference from their colleagues. It is in the nature of an innovation that at certain stages in its development within a school it will be very vulnerable to rejection.[3] This is particularly so if there is a general feeeling amongst staff that it has not justified its retention.

However there is another factor which affects the weight of resistance that an innovation must be able to withstand. Although I have argued that general staff reaction is important, the weight given to the views of particular subgroups within it will vary depending on the nature and extent of the proposed change. Roughly speaking the more widespread the effects that the change will create the greater the number of teachers outside the innovatory group who can (legitimately) claim to have a special interest in the future of the proposal. An innovation within a single subject area may be something requiring only the support of the teachers concerned and senior staff if it is to succeed. A proposal involving reblocking the timetable in larger units and forming an inter-departmental teaching team must convince far more staff of its validity before it can start. Furthermore it must be sufficiently successful to maintain such support when the time comes (as it almost inevitably will) for its continuation to be reconsidered.

It is clear that CSS in at least some of its variants, is an innovation that may require quite extensive changes of various kinds in a given school. To the extent that this is so, proportionally more staff will need to be convinced of its value. Nor is it sufficient to argue that it is demonstrably of *some* value. What has to be shown is that it is of *more* value than what must be foregone to accommodate it, and furthermore that the difference in value is sufficient to justify the extra short to medium term effort required to make the changes involved. The nature of the changes which a particular innovation may require can be grouped into five broad categories.

Firstly, a particular innovation may consist of changes in the content or teaching and learning methods used within a particular subject area to achieve given objectives more effectively, and/or revisions of assessment methods to help teachers get a better picture of the effects of a course of study they have been engaged in.

Secondly, some innovations require structural changes in a curriculum. These may include the introduction of new timetabled elements (such as Integrated Studies or Humanities), new methods of pupil grouping, or the formation of new teaching groups.

Thirdly, the innovation may involve a significant shift in the current balance of emphasis within the school between different categories of aims, promoting (for instance) 'social' as against 'academic' aims, or vice versa.

Fourthly, an innovation may involve the redistribution of desirable resources between different teachers, as individuals or groups. These resources include:

— finance,
— timetable time,
— accommodation, equipment and books,
— additional staffing,
— the opportunity to teach (or to avoid teaching!) particular categories of pupils,
— promotion prospects,
— access to positions on important decision-making groups within the staff.

Finally, really radical innovations may require a partial restructuring of the decision-making system of the school, not just altering which staff occupy which roles within it. In addition it is worth noting that one of the most important hidden costs of an innovation is the amount of a staff's policy-making deliberations it uses up, at the expense of other matters which might be brought under review.

Cutting across all these aspects of innovation is what we might call role innovation. In any school there is a working distribution of roles between all those involved, including teachers, pupils, senior staff, parents, ancillary workers, governors and so forth. Such roles will, at any given time, be more or less successfully inter-related so as to promote the successful achievement of the school's puposes. Thus the

organisation of teachers into departmental or faculty groupings represents not only a tacit allocation of educational responsibilities between different staff, but also defines to some extent a given teacher's role in relation to colleagues, parents, pupils and other groups concerned. Similarly, the way in which pupils are grouped affects the range of roles available to particular individuals (both teachers and pupils), and creates certain expectations on both sides concerning teacher/pupil relationships within a given timetabled element of the curriculum. Again, the distribution of control over curriculum decision-making (for instance the degree of autonomy a teacher has to negotiate the content and objectives of his or her teaching with the pupils concerned) also involves a particular conception of the role relationships between all those involved. Given all this, it seems a safe assumption that curriculum innovation of any significance will almost always create changes in teacher role, and that for the teachers affected this, together with issues concerning resource allocation, may be the most important aspects of the innovation.

So far then, I have argued that the difficulty of introducing an innovation into a school's curriculum is proportionate to the degree to which there are mismatches between the educational values of influential staff and those embodied in the innovation, and also that resistance will be proportionate to the amount of general curricular change required to incorporate the innovation, particularly in relation to resource allocation and teacher role and status.

If that is accepted we can get a crude but useful grip upon the problem of resistance to innovation by asking: which of the many elements in the curriculum discussed above is the one that is most crucially involved in determining educational ethos, resource allocation and teacher role and status?

No single factor is absolutely dominant in relation to a school's policy on these issues but arguably one internally complex element has a significance that far outstrips the others. That is the distribution of what we might call pupil subject hours. By this I mean the way in which the total of timetable time for different categories of pupils is distributed between the subjects on offer, where any timetable label (such as 'Humanities' or 'Counselling Time') is taken to refer either to a 'subject' or a conglomerate of subjects.

This distribution is of central importance in revealing the school's implicit philosophy because it indicates the relative importance given to different subjects and hence, by an indirect approximation, the relative significance given to different categories of aims. Similarly the degree of difference between subject time allocations to various categories of pupils (e.g. high as against low achievers or boys as against girls) gives us a crude index of the extent to which the school provides an homogenous as against a differentiated educational experience for pupils in these categories.

Similarly, the total of pupils hours covered by each subject is likely to give a rough index of the basic distribution of many other kinds of resource, such as space, staffing, finance, equipment and books. It is also likely to offer (albeit in an even rougher approximation still) some idea of promotion prospects and access to positions of decision-making power for members of different departments or faculties. (These factors are only very roughly correlated with the pupil subject hour total because, of course, some graded posts and decision-making roles in a large school are allocated on the basis of competences not connected with subject or faculty defined responsibilities.) The distribution of pupil hours between subject areas also sets obvious limits to the opportunities available for teachers within that subject area to teach particular categories of pupils.

Finally, although here the correlation is probably weakest, the total of pupil hours a subject commands is likely to have some relationship to its perceived status amongst teachers and pupils. This in turn may indirectly affect the status and self-image of members of a department, for whom the share of total pupil time their subject commands provides one index of its standing with both pupils and other teachers.

The claim for the central importance of the distribution of pupil time between subjects is speculative, although in many respects it could be checked quite easily in a particular school from available information. Nevertheless it seems a plausible assumption, and one which in turn suggests other hypotheses relevant to the innovation process, if we are prepared to make certain further assumptions (which can also be checked) concerning which categories of pupils teachers most prefer to teach. Here it might be worth taking as hypotheses that these preferences can, in most schools, be summarised as 'the brighter the better' and (more doubtfully) 'the older the better'. If these assumptions too are correct, we can then generate a number of hypotheses concerning which forms of innovations are likely (other things being equal) to generate least resistance. These hypotheses are:

1   A proposal for a new free-standing programme will encounter less resistance than it otherwise would if:
— it is introduced in a period when the total of pupil hours in the school is growing rather than static, or static rather than shrinking,
— it takes up the time of younger pupils rather than older ones,
— it takes up the time of low achieving rather than high achieving pupils,
— it is proposed as an extracurricular offering rather than a timetabled one,
—it is offered as an optional rather than as a compulsory programme,

— it is offered as a compulsory programme to replace all or part of another currently compulsory programme, rather than involving cutting down the time available for options by extending the compulsory core element in the timetable.

2   A proposal for an innovatory element wholly within an established subject will encounter less resistance that it otherwise would if:

— it is seen as a better way of achieving a currently accepted objective rather than as a proposal to divert pupil time to the pursuit of a new aim,

— insofar as there is internal resistance within the department to its introduction, it is offered to young low achieving pupils rather than others, in the extracurricular or optional areas of the departments work, rather than in the compulsory area (if any).

What light then does all this throw upon the question of introducing community service work into the curriculum? To some extent it provides an elaboration of the implicit conclusion drawn earlier (p. 68) that in general the Newsom variant is likely to be the most acceptable form of timetabled community service, and the Social Education Project the least. (Extracurricular variants, on this account, should be the most acceptable of all.)

But the account so far has been an essentially static one, presenting the problem as that of introducing a set innovation into a set curriculum at some specific instant in time. However, if we instead view the introduction of such an innovation as a process extending over a period of years then a rather different picture emerges. This developmental view has in my opinion been seriously undervalued by curriculum theorists, largely, I suspect, because most major innovations have been promoted by national project teams, working to create and introduce their proposals to schools within a relatively short time. Consequently for most of these teams a strategy of small scale introduction to a given school followed by a steady development of the innovation within the school was not an available option. Furthermore as much of the available literature and research on curriculum innovation in British schools has been centred around the histories of these

projects, the theories developed have tended to take the 'instant-impact' method of introducing an innovation as the obvious one. But if we consider instead the (largely unrecorded) processes by which schools naturally generate their own innovations, then a picture of gradual evolution (or, it must sometime be said, equally gradual decay) is, I suspect, a far more typical one.

If this is so it suggests a different way of viewing the whole problem. For rather than looking for some possibly non-existent way of introducing a full-blown CSS programme into a school overnight, supporters of CSS might instead look for a long-term strategy involving several stages by which the desired programme might be gradually developed.

In identifying the form that such a development strategy should take an innovator would be faced with three main tasks. The first would be to make a provisional identification of the long-term goal, in the form of a brief specification of the sort of CSS provision ultimately required and the basic aims it would have. The second would be to identify what sort of initial proposal would be both practicable and acceptable. The third task would be to establish some tentative picture of the line of development that could link the initial programme to the final version being envisaged.

This approach would appear to have a

number of distinct advantages for all concerned. Firstly it enables the teachers creating the programme to break down the practical problems involved into stages, solving them progressively over a period, rather than having to try to deal with all of them simultaneously from the very beginning. Given that most teachers working in this area are starting out as relative novices in some respects, that is a distinct benefit. Secondly, many senior staff might reasonably feel that it was a fair test of a group's genuine commitment to a new activity that they were prepared to view it as something to be developed steadily over time. Teachers who want to start from scratch with a Fifth Year examination course in Community Study/Service may be seen as being interested only in gaining some quick personal or professional boost from the innovation, rather than in making a serious job of it. Thirdly, the developmental approach recognises the legitimate right of other staff to see some real evidence of educational merit in the early stages of the development of such work before being required to sacrifice some of their own ambitions and plans in order to make space for the full-blown programme.

On the other hand, the innovating group would be entitled to expect fair dealing from colleagues in return for adopting this sort of approach. Firstly it would seem reasonable that they should not be encouraged to begin such a development if there is no willingness by other staff to accept their final goal, even in principle, from the start. If there is really no prospect of the final programme envisaged being accepted, then this should be clear from the outset. Secondly, it must be accepted that with this sort of innovation (as with many others) there may come a stage where the innovators see that their original endpoint is in some respects inadequate or inappropriate. If so, their new aspirations are entitled to a fair hearing. This is, of course, not to endorse the approach of an innovator who deliberately 'sells' his or her proposals under one label and then when the time is ripe tries to change tack to get what he or she really wanted in the first place. If, for instance, staff are persuaded from the beginning to accept community service solely as a way of gainfully occupying low achieving pupils, they cannot be blamed if they subsequently resist an attempt to turn it into an examination option that competes with their own subjects for high achievers too. On the other hand, if this development has been honestly presented as a serious possibility from the outset then objections in principle cannot appropriately be made at the end of the development sequence.

If then sequential development is accepted as the appropriate strategy in a given situation, can anything be said about what sequence of programmes it might be best to adopt?

The answer to this depends in part upon whether the strategy requires the development of community service as a minor integrated element within one or more conventional subjects, or its development as a timetabled subject in its own right.

The former pattern is one which has been endorsed by more than one prominent member of the community service movement outside the schools.[4] If (as the Balls' proposal envisaged) the final aim is to establish community service as an element in a range of subjects across the curriculum then presumably the best sequence of development would be one in which the introduction of the work into one subject would provide experience and evidence to make it easier for teachers in other subjects subsequently to experiment with the approach in their own areas. Such a development would be most effectively supported by the simultaneous extension of a job-finding and allocation system within the school, perhaps culminating in the designation of a specific member of staff as having some general responsibility for facilitating the work.

Whether such a strategy of piecemeal insemination would create the radical changes in the general ethos of a school that some of its supporters hope for is open to question. It seems equally probable that the widespread extension of community service work across the curriculum in this way could only follow, rather than precede, the evolution of a generally 'community-minded' ethos amongst staff as a whole. Furthermore it would be an educationally limited strategy insofar as the affective and skills aspect of the work would be likely to predominate, with only limited opportunities for creating a systematic social awareness in pupils through the work. However these criticisms, like so much else in this chapter, can only be speculative in the absence of any detailed studies of such strategies in action. On the other hand it could be claimed that this approach does utilise the relative autonomy of subject departments to insulate the innovation from any once-for-all rejection as a whole. Thus it may well represent a strategy which accepts certain limitations in its potential in return for definite gains. Furthermore its modular structure makes it relatively easy to adapt and adjust the line of

growth to fit changes in the general situation or policy of the school, unlike a more coherent and pre-planned strategy which may be seriously damaged by such changes.

The Newsom approach could either take the form of a particular variant on that already mentioned, or instead involve some sort of CSS course being proposed as a free-standing subject, to be permanently limited in practice largely to the lower achieving pupils. Here the question of a developmental strategy hardly arises (except of course in the different but important sense that any course requires internal evaluation and improvement as time goes by).

However if it were proposed to go for something more extensive in terms of the evolution of CSS as a free-standing subject, then the matter is more complex. On the basis of the discussion earlier in this chapter it would seem that in theory the best sequence of development here would be something like that shown in Diagram 6. But this may be mistaken, because the discussion so far has assumed that it is

Diagram 6 Hypothetical stages in development of CSS as a free-standing subject within a school's curriculum

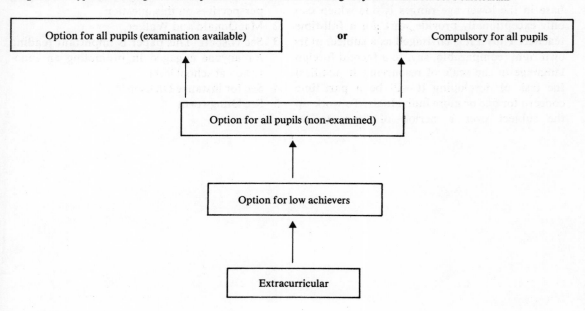

only the views of teachers about a proposed new programme that need to be considered. This is not entirely true even in the case of compulsory subjects. Where a programme is optional this assumption is self-evidently incorrect. Although teachers may decide upon the option structure and offer advice on which courses pupils should take, the views of parents and pupils are to varying degrees influential in the final decision. This is important because there are strong indications from a variety of sources that for the higher achieving pupils and their parents the effect of option choice upon their examination prospects is a major consideration. At a time of growing unemployment this concern is likely to increase, amongst teachers as much as others. Consequently it is probable that a line of development of the kind indicated would be likely to involve a different transition at the point where the programme moved towards becoming an option available to all pupils, unless definite steps were taken to deal with the problem. More seriously, there must be doubts about the long-term viability of this strategy in terms of staffing. The problem here is that an optional subject without a compulsory base in the lower age ranges is one which can only exceptionally provide work for a full-time teacher. Thus if it is envisaged as a subject in its own right (comparable, say, to a second foreign language in the scale of resourcing it justifies) the task of developing it will be a part-time concern for one or more individuals. To work up the subject over a period of years to an examinable option in such circumstances is difficult but not impossible.[5] To sustain it on that basis over several years would be very much more difficult again.

It would seem that all three of the basic innovation strategies described have their problems. None could be guaranteed to work, even in their own terms, in every situation. This would indicate that in practice the preliminary analysis of which strategy to adopt should focus very strongly upon the likely survival value of different versions of the innovation, with what would be the innovator's ideal taking an important but subsidiary role in the choice.

However it could be that a fourth strategy might be envisaged that, at least in many situations, could offer greater returns than any of these three. This possibility is one to which we will turn in the next chapter.

References

1 See for instance the works by Bernbaum, Peters, Watts, Richardson and Dickinson listed in the Bibliography, for varying perspectives on this question.
2 MacDonald and Walker.
3 See Nisbett. This paper is important reading for anyone engaged in promoting an innovation at school level.
4 See for instance Dickson.
5 See Dungworth

CHAPTER IX

SOCIAL EDUCATION IN THE 1980s
PREDICTIONS AND PROPOSALS

Two things at least can be learned from the history of secondary schools since the war. They are that changes in the wider social context have an important effect upon the schools, and that such change is always to be expected. The next decade is likely to confirm rather than refute both these claims. The question is what we can resonably predict about the form such changes will take, and what significance they may have for the future of social education in schools.

The present moment (early 1981) is hardly the best time to make such predictions, for the kinds of change that are flowing from the election of a Conservative government are by no means clear. Nevertheless, two other major underlying influences can already be felt in the schools and their possible impact considered.

The first is that there are as yet no signs that a significant upturn in Britain's economic performance can be expected in the next few years. This, together with the reality of a world recession in trade and the Conservative government's commitment to limiting public spending makes it clear that expenditure on education in real terms is very unlikely to rise.

Secondly, the demographic changes already apparent in the primary school population point to the 1980s being a decade of steady shrinkage in the school population in the 11 to 16 age range, amounting to a national reduction of something like a third over that period.

What is unclear is how national and local government bodies will react to the combined effects of financial stringency and demographic change. At one extreme the response could be to partially counter the demographic effect upon school numbers by raising the school leaving age to 17 or beyond. At the other extreme falling rolls might be directly matched by a proportionate reduction on spending on education, using the per-head expenditure in 1979 as the baseline from which such a reduction would be calculated.

Whatever particular policy within this range is adopted, several effects are likely,[1] at least in many schools in many local authorities. Thus:

1. Movement of staff between schools will slow down markedly, with staff staying longer in schools simply because promotion possibilities are far less than at present.
2. Local authorities will have to choose between closing complete schools, or reducing the size of those they have. Where particular schools are closed down there will probably be an intermediate phasing out period during which they will steadily decline in size.
3. In all schools in which pupil numbers are falling there will be pressure to drop high-cost optional subjects.
4. In such schools the combination of falling numbers and staff retirements will be likely to create staffing imbalances between different subject areas,

as the appointment of replacement staff will be very difficult to justify.

5   The combined effects of 1 and 4 will be to create pressures for teachers to teach more than one subject.

6   The combined effects of 3 and 5 may be to create a pressure towards consolidating a subject based curriculum into one made up of a much smaller number of core areas, taught by teams of teachers with interdisciplinary competences.

7   The merits of 'fringe' activities such as counselling, youth and community work, careers advice and pastoral care activities generally will come under close scrutiny, especially as the number of graded posts in a school begins to contract.

Clearly if such possibilities are actualised in anything like the form I have suggested, the consequences for social education work in the schools will be considerable.

Another area of likely change concerns the relationship between schools and outside groups. Accountability and community involvement are set fair to provide as important a set of challenges to the schools as falling rolls, although the form that these challenges will take is highly problematic.

On the one hand we might envisage a growth of central influence over the curriculum. The work of the Assessment of Performance Unit, a reorganised regional examination system and an increasing pressure from the centre for a nationally generated framework for a common core curriculum indicate the forms that such influence might take.

On the other hand there are signs of a rising pressure for greater involvement of parents and the local community in curriculum matters, and for the further development of community schools — a category which covers institutions with a multitude of aspirations, not all of them mutually compatible.

The final result of the interaction of all these different influences is impossible to predict. At one extreme it may produce the educationally destructive confrontations that have marked the attempts in nineteenth-century Britain[2] and contemporary America[3] to introduce rigid accountability schemes. Conversely, in the most optimistic view, there may be a significant gain in clarity about what can resonably be expected from the schools, and what kind of support they need (from both central and local government and the community) in order to achieve mutually agreed goals. Whatever the precise outcome (and it may well vary greatly from area to area and school to school) it is pretty clear that the present organisation of social education at every level is inadequate to meet the pressures that it will have to face.

In large part this is because the piecemeal development of this area of the curriculum has generally produced (at national, local and school level) a fragmented mosaic of educational activities. Nearly all of these are under resourced and under organised, individually providing only partial coverage of the educational objectives that a proper programme of social education would demand. In this respect Community Service is not untypical. Consequently it is one of a host of post-war innovations in this area that are likely to find the 1980s a time when they may have to struggle for a share of the steadily shrinking resources that will be available. Health Education, Social Studies, History, European Studies, Political Education, Civics, Moral Education, Humanities, Religious Education, Geography — the list of contenders for these resources lengthens almost yearly.

The irony of this situation is that the social tensions that have created the need for schools to take on a role in this area are quite likely to increase over the next decade. Alterations in the age structure of the population, technological change and political policies may well create increasing unemployment amongst the young and social polarization. Yet it is these same changes which may indirectly force schools away from a planned development of precisely that curriculum area in which a coherent educational response is needed to help young people to deal intelligently with the social issues that these changes create.

Where then does this leave Community Service work in particular? We have seen that in certain respects the Community Service movement has built up a substantial national and local framework to support the work in the schools. It has also been successful (although to precisely what degree is impossible to say) in recruiting teachers and others to run various types of timetabled programmes in the schools. This in turn has in some cases involved the creation of Community Study Service courses which can attract pupils across the whole achievement range. Where the movement's innovation strategy seems to me to be relatively weak is in the provision of teacher[4] training and of methods of assessment and evaluation for both pupils and programmes. Both of these weaknesses can arguably be traced to the way in which the innovation has largely developed outside the educational support and control system, within which much of the expertise and resources for providing these two elements is centred.

If one were to think in terms of promoting Community Study/Service as a free-standing subject, then it would be at these points that the innovation would seem to need consolidation, for without them it is difficult to see how the innovation could develop further, even if the next decade were to provide a context favourable to such growth.

The reason for this is that any educational activity which aspires to permanency in schools must evolve what may (at the risk of misunderstanding) be termed an educational tradition. By this I mean that an integrated body of concepts, methods and modes of evaluation and traditions of educational procedures must be established, which provides a rich concrete formulation of what the activity involves. In the creation of such a concrete tradition the tasks of developing teacher competence, methods of pupil assessment and of programme development are essential elements.

To speak here of a tradition is emphatically not to claim that a new educational activity must accommodate itself unresistingly to current educational conventions. Indeed were it to do so it would not be in any significant sense new. But it is to claim that successful innovation represents a more or less radical evolution within available curricular traditions, not a wholesale rejection of them.

Nor does the notion of a tradition involve assuming that the educational methods and ideas that the activity embodies must remain static. On the contrary, a sound tradition is based upon continuous evolutionary change. Once it becomes fixed in a particular format, its capacity to sustain imaginative teachers and to enable them to contribute to its subsequent development is arrested.

So should teacher development and improved evaluation methods be given priority? If so, it must be done in a way that takes note of the general problems that will face social education in the future, and also the doubts there must be about the long-term viability of CSS as a totally independent subject in schools.

My own view is that none of the three strategies described in previous chapters for extending community service work in schools is the best that can be envisaged, although all of them may be the best that can be achieved in some particular situation. What is needed is an attempt to integrate the teaching resources and support system that the advocates of community service work have built up into a more broadly conceived movement. This movement would have as its aim the creation and defence of a coherent tradition of social education provision within the education system, properly resourced, supported and recognised at every level.

If such a development came about it would do much to strengthen the claims of supporters of social education to an established place within a school's curriculum. At the same time it would much increase the capacity of its advocates at every level to support such claims in practice.

To attempt to outline the central objectives that such a tradition would need to pursue is beyond the scope of this book, as is a consideration of the considerable practical problems with which the proposal abounds. Its implementation would be much eased by a strong national initiative (which would not necessarily involve compulsion, uniformity or subsequent central direction). However if that were not forthcoming there would be much that could be done at the LEA level, [5] or even within individual schools to rationalise, consolidate and improve the overall provision of social education for pupils. Indeed, given the complexities and variability of contexts within which specific schools must operate, in this curriculum area above all there must be adequate room for school-based developmental research of the kind pioneered by the Humanities Curriculum Project[6] and subsequently by the Ford Teaching Project.[7] How to combine such a stance with the provision of adequate local and (if possible) national support structures is the central problem in the development of a creative tradition in social education.

Within such a framework the community service movement would have distinctive contributions to make. Its network of local support groups would provide a means of linking school and community that could provide advocates of such related innovations as Health and Moral Education and Social and Community Studies with access for pupils to real life situations of great educational value. The role of the movement's nationally generated teaching materials and dissemination network would again lend itself easily to expansion and integration within a wider framework of concerns. The possibilities too for LEA-supported in-service courses (perhaps with a range of specialisms within the general framework of social education) offers an equally obvious role for the movement.

In return, community service would have a clear potential location and role within a school's curriculum as part of a major unified curriculum area. This would avoid the risks of collapse associated with the one-teacher-subject approach. At the same time it would provide a tighter focus for productive interaction and progressive development (at national, local and school levels) than could be expected from the across-the-board approach that some of its supporters currently advocate.

To argue for the line of development that I am advocating is of course, to reject other possibilities. But it could be argued that the 1980s will be a period in which a commitment to clarity of pupose, a realistic focussing of effort and a certain kind of imaginative professionalism will be the key features that innovatory movements will require if they are to prosper. Speaking as a sympathetic outsider, I cannot myself see anything in the essential spirit behind community service work in schools that is incompatible with accepting such a commitment.

References

1 See Lightfoot, and Shaw for a fuller discussion of this.
2 See Matthew Arnold's reports and comments on the Revised Code reprinted in Sutherland.
3 See House.

4 As distinct from training for organisers, for
for which there already appears to be fairly
extensive provision; see National Youth
Bureau Induction Pack and their Annual
Report, for instance.

5 See for instance Mant, and Oliver.

6 See Stenhouse, chapters 9—11.

7 See Elliott and Adelman.

APPENDIX

Cambridgeshire Community Study/Service Project: Contract Between the Associate and the Authority

(1) *The Associate's Task*

The Associate's task is to prepare a general report (plus any necessary abstracts) for the Authority upon the problems and possibilities of secondary school-based Community/Study Service work. The purpose of this report is to assist the Authority in deciding upon its general policy in relation to this area of the curriculum.

(2) *The use to be made of data gained in schools*

The material upon which this report will be based will be gained largely from staff, pupils and others involved in, or directly affected by, Community Study/Service programmes in schools. In order to obtain an accurate picture of their views it is essential that anyone providing information or opinions should be satisfied that their views will be treated with whatever degree of confidentiality they wish. To ensure this, the Associate's work will be conducted in accordance with the following rules:

(*a*) Informal conversations or comments will be treated as strictly confidential, and will not be referred to in any way in the final report.

(*b*) Formal expressions of views (e.g. replies to questionnaires or comments made in taped interviews) will also be strictly confidential. However the Associate may, with the explicit permission of the person concerned, use such material in an anonymous form in the report where this seems desirable.

(*c*) The purpose of the visits to schools is *not* to evaluate or pass judgment upon the particular programmes being developed, but to try to identify the general issues that CSS work raises and to try to understand how different people see this work. Consequently, the Associate will not offer opinions on the programmes to those involved, to other staff in the school, or to outsiders.

(*d*) The Associate will not comment (either in the report or in informal conversation), upon the programmes of individual schools, or upon the work of staff or pupils within them.

(3) *The report and its preparation*

The report will be submitted to the Authority by September 1977 at the latest.

Before final submission, the following procedure will be followed:

The Associate will prepare a draft version. This will be circulated to the members of the Officials/Heads Committee. At this stage they will be concerned only to check that the Report contains no quotations or comments that could be traced to, or read as comments upon, any identifiable school or individual. Should any such material be found it will be deleted or rewritten.

The copies of the report will then be forwarded to the Heads of schools visited and to the Homerton Study Group for discussion. Nobody will be allowed to delete or amend items in the Report, but anyone who wishes to submit additional or alternative comments, criticisms or policy proposals will be entitled to do so. Such comments, provided they are of reasonable length, will then be added to the original report as a separate section. Both report and comments will then be submitted to the Authority.

(4) *Independent validation of the report*

The measures taken to protect confidentiality will mean that the Authority will be unable to check directly that the Associate has given a fair and correct account of the issues that CSS work involves. (They will not, for instance, be able to check anonymous quotations directly against the original data, or to see if the Associate has been unacceptably selective in his choice of quotations.) Nor could other curriculum research workers check this. However it is possible to maintain confidentiality and still provide an independent check upon the report's validity.

To do this, should it be thought desirable, the Authority and the Associate should agree upon a mutually acceptable independent research worker with relevant experience. He would then be given both the report and all the collected data upon which it was based and could, if required, confirm that the report was valid, without revealing any details of the original data. When collecting data the Associate will make clear to those interviewed that this may be done. Should such independent validation be required, the Authority would be responsible for any fees or expenses involved.

(5) *Dissemination, publication and copyright*

Copyright of the report will rest with the Authority, as will decisions concerning possible dissemination and publication. It is possible that the Associate will wish to publish work arising from experience gained in connection with the Project. The copyright of such publications will remain with the Associate. Where such publications involve no direct reference to the Project or the Authority as such, the Associate will be allowed to publish as he sees fit. However, if any proposed publication includes any direct reference to the Authority or the Project, then the Associate must first submit it for approval to the Officials/Heads Committee, or their representative. They may either refuse permission to publish at all, or require alterations before publication.

BIBLIOGRAPHY

Readers who wish to get a fuller picture of community service work in practice will find Mog Ball's *Young People as Volunteers* an excellent source. A very useful guide to other sources of information is *The School in Action,* edited by Ann Griffith and Chris Moffat. Up to date information about what is available can be obtained from:

Community Service Volunteers
237 Pentonville Road
London N1 9NJ
Tel. 01-278 6601

A great deal of relevant material is published in the journal *Youth in Society,* produced by the National Youth Bureau. (Some of the articles I have found most helpful are listed in the bibliography below.)

A useful starting point for exploring the relevance of general curriculum theory to the issues I have discussed would be to look at the books by Lawrence Stenhouse and Barry MacDonald and Rob Walker. They give extensive further references.

Ball, C. and Ball, M., *Education for a change.* Harmondsworth: Penguin, 1973.

Ball, C., *Community service and the young unemployed.* Leicester: National Youth Bureau, 1977.

Ball, M., *Young people as volunteers.* Berkhampsted: The Volunteers Centre, 1976.

Ball, M., 'Community service for all?' in *Youth in Society,* No. 22, March/April 1977.

Bantock, G. H., 'Towards a theory of popular education', *Times Educational Supplement,* 12 and 19 March 1971. Reprinted in Golby, M. *et al.*

Benn, C. and Simon, B., *Half way there: report on the British comprehensive school reform* (2nd edition). Harmondsworth: Penguin, 1972.

Bernbaum, G. (with the assistance of Davis, D.), 'The role of the head' in Peters, R. S.

Birtwistle, A., 'Project trident and work experience' in *Youth in Society,* No. 7, September/October 1974.

Calvocoressi, P., *The British experience 1945-75.* London: Bodley Head, 1978

Cheetham, N., 'Volunteers or responsible citizens?' in *Youth in Society,* No. 23.

Dickinson, N. B., 'The head teacher as innovator: a study of an English School District' in Reid, W. A. and Walker, D. F.

Dickson, A., 'An opportunity for all?' in Griffith, A. and Moffat, C.

Dungworth, M., 'Six good reasons for avoiding community service' in Griffith, A. and Moffat, C.

Elliott, J. and Adelman, C., 'Innovation at the classroom level: a case study of the Ford Teaching Project' (Unit 28, Open University Course E203, *Curriculum design and development*). Milton Keynes: Open University Press, 1976.

Elliot, J. and Pring, R., *Social Education and social understanding.* London: University of London Press, 1975.

Genasci, S., 'The Watford Social Education Project' in *Youth in Society,* No. 25, October 1977.

Golby, M., Greenwald, J. and West, R. (eds) *Curriculum design.* London: Croom Helm, 1975.

Griffith, A. and Moffat, C. (eds) *The School in Action.* London: C.S.V., 1977.

Hargreaves, D., *Social relations in a second-*

ary school. London: Routledge and Kegan Paul, 1967.

Hargreaves, D., *Interpersonal relations and education.* London: Routledge and Kegan Paul, 1972.

Harris, A., Lawn, M. and Prescott, W. (eds), *Curriculum innovation.* London: Croom Helm, 1975.

Hooper, R., 'Educational technology in the USA—a diagnosis of failure' in *Audio-Visual Communication Review,* Vol. 17, No. 3, 1969. Reprinted in Hooper, R. (ed.) *The curriculum: context, design and development.* Edinburgh: Oliver and Boyd, 1971.

House, E. R., 'Accountability in the USA' in *Cambridge Journal of Education,* Vol. 5, No. 2, 1975.

Humble, S. and Simons, H., *From council to classroom: an evaluation of the diffusion of the Humanities Curriculum Project.* London: Macmillan Educational, 1978.

Kerry, J., 'Doing a Trident: coordinated work experience schemes' in *Trends 1979,* No. 2, Summer 1979.

Lightfoot, M., 'The educational consequences of falling rolls' in Richards, C.

MacDonald, B. and Walker, R., *Changing the curriculum.* London: Open Books, 1976.

Mant, J., 'No soft option . . . the B.Y.V. education function' in *Youth in Society,* No. 17, May/June 1976.

Merson, M. W. and Campbell, R. J., 'Community education: instruction for inequality' in *Education for Teaching,* Spring 1974. Reprinted in Golby, M. *et al.*

Morris, H., *The Village College* (2nd edition). Cambridge: Cambridge University Press, 1925. Reprinted in Rée.

Musgrave, P. W. *The moral curriculum: a sociological analysis.* London: Methuen, 1978.

National Working Party of Young Volunteer Organisers, *Young Volunteer Work— philosophy, practice and needs.* Leicester:

National Youth Bureau, n.d.

National Youth Bureau, *Fifth Annual Report.* Leicester: National Youth Bureau, 1978.

National Youth Bureau, *Induction Pack.* Leicester: National Youth Bureau, 1979.

Newson Report, *Half our Future.* A report of the Central Advisory Council for Education (England). London: HMSO, 1963

Nisbett, J., 'Innovation—bandwagon or hearse?' *Bulletin of Victorian Institute of Educational Research,* No. 33, 1974. Reprinted in Harris, A. *et al.*

Oliver, J., 'The development of B.Y.V.'s educational work: a teacher's point of view' in *Youth in Society,* No. 17, May/June, 1976.

Peters, R. S. (ed.), *The role of the head.* London: Routledge and Kegan Paul, 1976.

Peters, R. S., 'The contemporary problem' (Introduction to Peters, R. S. (ed.) *The role of the head*)

Rée, H., *Educator extraordinary: the life and achievement of Henry Morris.* London: Longman, 1973.

Reid, W. A. and Walker, D. F. (eds), *Case studies in curriculum change.* London: Routledge and Kegan Paul, 1975.

Rennie, J., 'Community and curriculum' in *Youth in Society,* No. 25, October 1977.

Rennie, J., Lunzer, E. A. and Williams, W. T., *Social education: an experiment in secondary schools* (Schools Council Working Paper No. 51). London: Evans Methuen Educational, 1974.

Richards, C. (ed.) *Power and the curriculum: issues in curriculum studies.* Driffield: Nafferton Books, 1978.

Richardson, E., *The teacher, the school and the task of management.* London: Heinemann, 1973.

Schon, D. A., *Beyond the stable state: public and private learning in a changing society.* Harmondsworth: Penguin, 1971.

Scrimshaw, P. 'The language of social education' in Elliot, J. and Pring, R.

Scrimshaw, P. 'Towards the whole curriculum' (Unit 9 in the Open University Course E203 *Curriculum design and development*). Milton Keynes: Open University Press, 1976.

Scrimshaw, P., 'Illuminative evaluation: some reflections' in *Journal of Further and Higher Education,* Vol. 3, No. 2, Summer 1979.

Shaw, K., 'Managing the curriculum in contraction' in Richards, C.

Shipman, M., *Inside a curriculum project.* London: Methuen, 1974.

Slough, C., 'Planning an exam course' in Griffith, A. and Moffat, C.

Stenhouse, L., *An introduction to curriculum research and development.* London: Heinmann, 1975.

Sugarman, B., *The school and moral development.* London: Croom Helm, 1973.

Sutherland, G., *Arnold on education.* Harmondsworth: Penguin, 1973.

Swain, G., 'Community service to the rescue' in *Youth in Society,* No. 14, November/December 1975.

Taylor, K., 'Community education: a multi-disciplinary approach' in *Youth in Society,* No. 23, May/June 1977.

Tyler, W. R., *Basic principles of curriculum and instruction.* Chicago: University of Chicago Press, 1949.

Walker, R., and MacDonald, B., 'Curriculum innovation at school level' (Unit 27 in Open University Course E203, *Curriculum design and development*). Milton Keynes: Open University Press, 1976.

Watts, J., 'Sharing it out: the role of the head in participatory government', in Peters, R. S.

Wiseman, S. and Pidgeon, D., *Curriculum evaluation.* Windsor: N.F.E.R., 1970.

Woodward, F., *Case study — Youth Action Cambridge.* Leicester: National Youth Bureau, 1979.

Young Volunteers Resource Unit, 'Young volunteer organisations' in Griffith, A. and Moffat, C.